"I THINK I FIGURED IT OUT," MORGAN SAID AS he stopped directly in front of her.

Maddie watched his lips move, but didn't understand a word he was saying. She wanted what her dreams had teased and tempted her with. She wanted Morgan to kiss her. "What did you figure out?"

His hand cupped her cheek and she forgot to breathe. His gaze roamed her face as if he were memorizing every detail. "Underneath that modern appearance of a very independent and worldly woman, you possess an old-fashioned heart."

She blinked. "Old-fashioned?" No one had ever applied that description to her before. She didn't want to be old-fashioned. She wanted to be sophisticated and brave and seductive. She wanted to seduce Morgan into kissing her.

His thumb softly stroked her lower lip. "There's nothing wrong with an old-fashioned heart, Maddie." He lowered his head and brushed a kiss where his thumb had just caressed. "In fact, I'm becoming very fond of one in particular."

WHAT ARE *LOVESWEPT* ROMANCES?

They are stories of true romance and touching emotion. We believe those two very important ingredients are constants in our highly sensual and very believable stories in the LOVESWEPT line. Our goal is to give you, the reader, stories of consistently high quality that may sometimes make you laugh, sometimes make you cry, but are always fresh and creative and contain many delightful surprises within their pages.

Most romance fans read an enormous number of books. Those they truly love, they keep. Others may be traded with friends and soon forgotten. We hope that each LOVESWEPT romance will be a treasure—a "keeper." We will always try to publish

LOVE STORIES YOU'LL NEVER FORGET BY AUTHORS YOU'LL ALWAYS REMEMBER

The Editors

White Lace & Promises:

HERE'S LOOKIN' AT YOU

MARCIA EVANICK

BANTAM BOOKS
NEW YORK · TORONTO · LONDON · SYDNEY · AUCKLAND

WHITE LACE & PROMISES: HERE'S LOOKIN' AT YOU
A Bantam Book / October 1997

LOVESWEPT and the wave design are registered trademarks of Bantam Books, a division of Bantam Doubleday Dell Publishing Group, Inc. Registered in U.S. Patent and Trademark Office and elsewhere.

All rights reserved.
Copyright © 1997 by Marcia Evanick.
Cover art copyright © 1997 by Aleta Jenks.
No part of this book may be reproduced or transmitted in any form or by any means, electronic or mechanical, including photocopying, recording, or by any information storage and retrieval system, without permission in writing from the publisher.
For information address: Bantam Books.

If you purchased this book without a cover you should be aware that this book is stolen property. It was reported as "unsold and destroyed" to the publisher and neither the author nor the publisher has received any payment for this "stripped book."

ISBN 0-553-44587-1

Published simultaneously in the United States and Canada

Bantam Books are published by Bantam Books, a division of Bantam Doubleday Dell Publishing Group, Inc. Its trademark, consisting of the words "Bantam Books" and the portrayal of a rooster, is Registered in U.S. Patent and Trademark Office and in other countries. Marca Registrada. Bantam Books, 1540 Broadway, New York, New York 10036.

PRINTED IN THE UNITED STATES OF AMERICA

OPM   10 9 8 7 6 5 4 3 2 1

PROLOGUE

Morgan De Witt parked his car directly in front of the White Lace and Promises Bridal Boutique and eyed the elegant store thoughtfully. His sister, Georgia, whom he was picking up for their lunch date, was in there having a final fitting on her wedding gown. He had done it! At thirty-two Georgia was finally getting married and relieving him of his sense of responsibility toward his little sister. He couldn't have picked a better man for Georgia than Adam Young. Adam was a decent man, well respected, and wealthy enough to keep his sister financially secure if she ever decided to give up her antique business.

Sixteen years earlier, when he was twenty-two and had just graduated from college, their parents were in a car accident. Their mother had been killed instantly, but their father had lasted for five hours, long enough for his children to make it to his bedside, and for Franklin De Witt to extract a promise from his son. Franklin wanted Morgan to raise his sixteen-year-old sister and to make sure she found happiness in life. Morgan would have taken care of his sister no matter what, but the promise he had sworn to his father had lain heavily on his mind these past years. Finally, Georgia was going to march down the aisle toward her happiness and he would be free to pursue his own.

The family home, on the outskirts of Lancaster, Pennsylvania, was going to seem awfully empty without Georgia. Maybe it was time to find himself a wife and start a family. After all, he was thirty-eight years old and not getting any younger. Georgia was going to be too busy with her own life and husband to act as his hostess when he needed one.

Shaking his head at his absurd thoughts, he got out of the car and headed for the shop. Imagine him, the lone wolf of the country club set, looking for a competent hostess and wife! He would have laughed, except somewhere deep down inside he felt the familiar ache of loneliness. The ache had been growing stronger these past few years. He forced himself to smile as he opened the shop door. He would have plenty of time to worry about his own future after he had seen to Georgia's.

His smile disappeared as he glanced around the elegant boutique. Something was wrong. Three of Georgia's bridesmaids, in various stages of dress, were huddled around a rose-colored curtain at the rear of the shop. A woman with a pincushion strapped to her forearm was dabbing at tears, and Cleo Bodine, the owner of the exclusive boutique, was wringing her hands. "What's going on?" he asked. Georgia was nowhere in sight.

Georgia's friend Vanessa, who was dressed in a yellow gown and crying her eyes out, dashed across the room and threw herself into his arms. He sighed and rolled his eyes as her body slammed into his, forcing him to take a step back. Vanessa made a habit of throwing herself at him no matter what the circumstances. He would have found it flattering if it wasn't so damn annoying. He carefully but firmly held her away from his chest. "Vanessa, where's Georgia?"

Brown curls bobbed in the direction of the curtain. "She's in the fitting room with Adam."

He ignored her delicate sniffles. "Adam? What's he doing here? Isn't it bad luck for the groom to see the bride in her dress before the wedding?"

"That's what I told him, but I guess it was too late."

"What do you mean?" He frowned at the curtain.

"Adam just called off the wedding."

He released Vanessa so quickly, she almost tripped over the hem of her gown, and he marched toward the dressing room. His grip was so fierce he nearly pulled the curtain from its rings as he barged into the room. "What in the hell is going on in here?" he demanded. "Vanessa just told me you're calling off the wedding, Young!"

Georgia stepped in front of Adam. "Now, Morgan," she began.

He noticed the moisture pooling in her china-blue eyes and felt like strangling Adam Young. For sixteen years he had protected his little sister. He didn't think he could shield her from this heartache, but he could try. He gently moved her to one side and faced the man who had made her cry. "Did you or did you not call off the wedding, Young?"

He ignored the tender look Adam gave Georgia before the other man squared his shoulders and faced Morgan. "I called off the wedding, Morgan."

Morgan's fist shot out, connecting with Adam's face with a resounding thud. Satisfaction pulsed through his body as Adam flew backward and landed in a pile of lace and silk. He had never hit another man before. He abhorred violence of any kind, but that one punch had felt marvelous. His fist screamed in agony, making him wonder if he had just broken a few knuckles, but it was well worth it for what Adam had put Georgia through and for ruining Morgan's own fanciful dreams of finding someone to ease his loneliness.

He heard Georgia cry out, saw her take a step toward Adam. He quickly grabbed her wrist and dragged her from the room, still wearing her gown. Adam, the heartbreaking scum, didn't deserve her concern. Morgan's whole future, or lack of one, had been hanging on this wedding. Adam Young should count his blessings that he didn't hit him again just for the hell of it.

ONE

Morgan De Witt pulled onto the circular brick drive and parked behind an aged green van. He hadn't expected Madeline Andrews to be driving a van, and an old one at that. He had pictured Glen's daughter whizzing around the country in some snappy little sports car, not a van that looked like it should have a plumber's name painted on the side. He wearily rubbed the back of his neck where a knot had taken up permanent residence and glanced at his watch. Nine-thirty at night was on the late side, but not too late. Lights were burning in quite a few of the rooms in Glen's house.

The last two days had been hell. He had been running on pure adrenaline and a few catnaps. He was ready to crash. But he had one thing left to do before heading home and reacquainting himself with his bed. He had promised Glen that he would make sure Maddie was all right. Morgan shook his head. Glen was worried about his daughter when he should be worrying about his own health. Maddie was thirty-two years old and had been living on her own since college, while Glen had just suffered a stroke. Granted, it was a mild stroke, but a stroke all the same.

Glen Andrews had always treated him like a son, and Morgan would do everything in his power to shoulder Glen's worries and make sure he got the rest he needed. Glen had said he would rest better knowing Morgan was checking on Maddie.

He had missed Maddie at the hospital by ten minutes. Glen had told him she had arrived in mid-afternoon and hadn't left her father's side until Glen had insisted she go home and get some rest. Glen's speech was still slurred, but Morgan had had a good chuckle when Glen said that Maddie looked like hell. The last time he had seen Maddie, which was about two years ago, it would have taken a train wreck to make her look anything but gorgeous. If she hadn't headed right back to wherever she had been living at the time, he might have disregarded the fact that Glen was more like a father than a business associate to him and asked the fiery redhead out to dinner.

Morgan gave up on the knotted mass of tension in his neck and got out of the car. A hot shower and six hours of sleep would do wonders both for his mind and his body. As always, he admired Glen's magnificent brick home as he made his way up the paved walk and rang the doorbell. The house had been in the Andrews family since before the Civil War and its simple elegance never ceased to amaze him. Every generation had done its part of adding the latest in modern conveniences, but the charm of the house had never been compromised.

The last chime of the bell faded in the depths of the house and he thought he heard a voice. He gave Maddie a minute to answer the door, and when she didn't, he pressed the bell again. This time he listened more closely. Definitely a voice, but it didn't sound like Maddie.

He had talked to her on the phone the day before because he'd had the job of notifying her about her father's stroke. Her tone had gone from curious, to shocked, to tearful, and eventually to a calm acceptance, after he convinced her that her father was in good hands and the prognosis was for a full recovery. In all that range of emotion, her voice hadn't hit the pitch he'd just heard.

The voice called, "Come in." Morgan frowned at the door. Maybe Maddie wasn't alone. All he'd known was she was coming home. He hadn't bothered to ask if she was coming alone. It wasn't any of his business, even if she'd brought the entire acting company she was currently employed with. But it *was* his concern if whoever had come with her invited just anyone, sight unseen, into the house. This was one of the safest neighborhoods in the county, but still, a little common sense was called for. He sure as hell didn't want to be the one to tell Glen that something had happened to his precious little girl.

He raised his hand and pounded on the door. The voice once again called for him to enter. He couldn't even detect the sound of footsteps coming toward the door. Was Maddie that unconcerned for her safety? He grasped the doorknob and frowned as it turned in his hand and the door swung open. He stepped into the empty foyer and closed the door behind him. No one called out to him.

"Maddie?" He didn't want to go barging in on her if she wasn't aware of his arrival. But he was positive he'd heard someone call for him to come in.

"Be quiet!" someone screamed in a high-pitched voice from the room on his right. He froze in his tracks, staring into the room. He couldn't see anyone. "Or the dame gets it!" another voice growled. What in the world was going on? He inched his way closer and peeked into the well-lit room.

He couldn't see anyone, only two large birdcages, each containing a brilliantly colored green parrot. He stepped into the room. "Maddie?"

"You dirty rat!" one parrot snarled at him. The bird sounded like James Cagney with a sore throat.

"Wanna boogie?" the other parrot asked.

Here's Lookin' at You
11

He chuckled and shook his head. So this was who had invited him in, parrots! He wondered where Maddie was, and if she knew the front door was unlocked. "Hello, fellows. Where's Maddie?" He approached the cages cautiously. He didn't know the first thing about parrots, or any other bird for that matter. The only thing he knew was the parrots weren't Glen's.

One of the birds clung to the brass bars and poked his bill out between the rails. "Plant one on me!" The yellowish bill continued to move and a noise that sounded like huge, smacking kisses emerged from the parrot's throat.

Morgan rolled his eyes and turned toward the other parrot, who was gazing at him with unblinking eyes. "What do you have to say?"

"Sinners repent!"

"Dirty coppers!"

"Walk the plank, graaawwwk, walk the plank!"

"Disco's dead."

"Evermore, graaawwwk, evermore!"

He scowled, having had enough of the squawking that made absolutely no sense. "Shut up, before I make parrot soup out of you both."

"Maddie loves me! Maddie loves me!"

"So, just because you're Maddie's birds doesn't mean you won't look good floating in a pot of noodles and vegetables."

"Really, Morgan," said Madeline Andrews as she entered the room, "must you threaten my poor defenseless pets?"

He turned toward the door, his scowl deepening. Maddie was dressed in a light green robe with huge, puffy yellow flowers splashed all over it. Her hair was damp. The moisture had darkened the red curls to a deep mahogany. She apparently had just stepped out of the shower, which would explain why she hadn't heard the doorbell. "Your defenseless pets just invited a total stranger into the house." He glared once more at the birds before turning back toward her. "Did you know that the front door was unlocked?"

"That was my doing and I can assure you José and Manuel had nothing to do with that." She walked over to the nearest cage and smiled. "Has José been a naughty bird?"

"Naughty bird, grrraaawwwk, naughty bird."

Maddie chuckled and moved to the other cage. "What about you, Manuel? Have you been a bad boy?"

Manuel nodded his head as he squawked, "Bad boy, bad boy."

"Yes, you are, but I still love you both." She glanced between the two cages. "José and Manuel, I want you to apologize to Morgan. Say you are sorry."

"Sorry," cried Manuel.

"No way, José," screeched José.

"José, is that any way to treat a guest?"

"Be our guest! Be our guest!" answered the green-feathered underfed chicken.

Here's Lookin' at You

"José, say you're sorry or it will be curtains for you."

"Curtains for you!" José made a choking noise that sounded amazingly like someone was wringing his little neck. Morgan couldn't help but smile at the prospect.

"José, say you're sorry."

"Sorry, grrraaawwwk, sorry."

"That's a good boy," Maddie said.

"Good boy," cried José.

"Pretty boy," added Manuel.

Maddie laughed and shook her head. "See, Morgan, they're just harmless little chatterboxes."

He didn't see anything of the kind. Harmless wasn't one of the adjectives he would use to describe the green monsters. Both of the parrots had a look in their eyes that said if they weren't behind bars, they would love nothing better than to peck his eyes out. "They should be muzzled."

"Was there a reason you stopped by, besides to insult my pets?"

"Your father wanted me to make sure you were okay and settled in."

"As you can see, I'm fine. This is the house I grew up in. I don't think I need to settle into it."

He studied her pale complexion and the dark circles beneath her emerald-green eyes. Glen was right, she did look like hell. Or at least like someone who hadn't gotten a lot of sleep the night before and had driven most of the day to get to her father's side. His glance slid from her damp hair to the bare toes peeking out from beneath the awful-looking robe. Maddie was still one gorgeous woman and it was going to take more than a few lost hours of sleep to change that. "You look like hell."

"Gee, Morgan, so nice of you to notice." She walked out of the room.

He stared at the empty doorway for a moment. Lord, even the back of that hideous robe had those puffy flowers. Maddie could have gained twenty pounds since the last time he saw her and he wouldn't be able to tell under that bulky garment. He expected to hear the front door open, but instead she headed for the kitchen at the back of the house. He could leave now, with a clear conscience. Maddie was okay and appeared to be settled in quite nicely. But there had been something in her tear-swollen eyes that compelled him to stay.

Maddie needed a friend right now.

He knew he didn't qualify as a true friend, but he was the only one there. Sighing heavily, he headed for the doorway and was brought up short by a piercing catcall from Manuel. He turned around and glowered at the bird.

Manuel tilted his head, whistled once again, and said, "Nice butt."

He was unsure if he wanted to laugh or toss the damn bird out the window. Instead he looked at José, who seemed to be enjoying his indecision.

Here's Lookin' at You

"What, no comment from the other member of the peanut gallery?"

José just tilted his head, remaining silent. Satisfied he had finally gotten some respect, Morgan started to leave again. He was nearly through the doorway when José cried out, "Hamster brain."

He kept on going toward the kitchen, positive his laughter would only encourage the little monsters. He really had to find out from Maddie what in the world had possessed her to teach those two such things.

He found her in the kitchen, standing at a counter and staring down at a casserole dish. Tears were slowly rolling down her cheeks and plopping onto the note she had clutched in her hand. As soon as she noticed him, she wiped at her eyes with the sleeve of the robe. He glanced around the room, couldn't see any tissues, so he ripped off two paper towels and thrust them into her hand. "Stop your blubbering."

Her glare was murderous, but at least she stopped crying. He didn't know what to do with a crying woman. On the rare occasion when his sister had cried, he had given her whatever she wanted. When other women tried tears to get their way, it only made him mad. Maddie's tears weren't for things she couldn't have. They were for her father and the worry she had been living with for the past thirty hours.

He picked up the note she had dropped and quickly scanned it. It was from Glen's housekeeper. She had come in that morning and readied Maddie's room and prepared her a quick dinner. Her prayers were also expressed.

He lifted the lid of the casserole and sniffed. "She can't be that bad of a cook, can she?"

"Ethel is a wonderful cook." Maddie picked up the dish and placed it in the microwave. After pushing a few buttons to start it, she noisily blew her nose, tossed the used paper towel into the trash, and turned to face him. "I thought you were leaving."

"Your birds insulted me again."

"I'm sure you must have said something to deserve it."

He glanced at the four cardboard boxes crowded onto the kitchen table. One contained bird food. Square boxes, glass jars, and plastic containers of every conceivable type of bird food ever made. José and Manuel were obviously very pampered pets. The other boxes appeared to contain an assortment of everything from crackers to aluminum foil. "You sure pack a lot for a quick trip home."

"It's not a quick trip. I'm here to stay." She opened a cabinet and reached for a plate. "My father would be appalled if I didn't invite you to stay and share Ethel's famous sausage and potato casserole with me."

"If that's an invitation, I accept." He had skipped his own dinner to get to the hospital before visiting hours ended. He had barely made the

Here's Lookin' at You

last five minutes of visiting hours, and then had to persuade some marine drill sergeant of a nurse to let him stay a little longer. There was no casserole waiting for him in his refrigerator. If he was lucky he'd find some leftovers he could slap between two pieces of bread. The delicious aroma pouring from the microwave was just too tempting to pass up.

Maddie didn't bother to hide her sigh of resignation as she took down another plate. "I better warn you now that I won't be much company." She carefully arranged the plates on the breakfast counter, where there were two stools. "I'll probably fall asleep in the middle of talking."

"That's understandable." He nodded toward the boxes. "What do you mean you're home for good? What about your job and apartment?"

"The play I was in went on without me last night, just like it will go on without me for the remainder of the run. My understudy was grinning the whole time she was offering her blessings for my father's speedy recovery."

"Nice woman."

Maddie shrugged. "It's the business." She opened the refrigerator and frowned. "What do you want, milk, cola, or orange juice? There's some red wine, too, but I don't think we should be having that. One glass of wine and I'll be falling asleep in my dinner plate and you would be stuck carrying me upstairs to bed." She turned and glanced at him. "And just for the record, you don't look any better than I feel."

He only grunted at her observation. He had a mirror; he knew what he looked like. "Milk will be fine." The prospect of carrying Maddie to bed wasn't that daunting, he mused. In fact, it held a variety of intriguing possibilities.

Two minutes later they were sitting side by side at the counter, the steaming casserole dish between them. Maddie served herself, then handed him the large spoon.

He had to smile at the picture she made sitting there in that ridiculous robe. It covered her from the base of her throat to her ankles. There was not one alluring thing about the garment. So why was it driving him crazy? He would give a lot to know what she was wearing beneath it, or if she was wearing anything at all.

He watched as she dug into her meal, thinking that he had never shared dinner with a woman while she was wearing a robe. A few breakfasts over the years, sure, but never dinner. He chuckled at the memory of some of his breakfast companions' robes. Not a one was constructed with more fabric than his couch.

"What's so funny?"

"Nothing." He didn't think she would appreciate the humor in the situation. "Glen looks a lot better tonight than he did yesterday."

"Then I don't even want to think about what he might have looked like yesterday." Maddie toyed with a piece of potato. "I want to thank you, Morgan, for being here when my father needed someone."

"You don't need to thank me, Maddie. Glen's always been around when I needed him." He placed his fork on his near-empty plate. "Does your father know you're home for good?"

"Not yet. I didn't want to start an argument while he's still in the hospital. I would appreciate it if we can keep it our little secret for now."

"Your father loves you, Maddie. He'll be thrilled when he finds out you're staying here."

"Dad wants me to follow my dreams, Morgan." She cut a hunk of sausage into six microbites. "I don't want to add the guilt of me moving back home on his shoulders."

"Maybe he won't see it as guilt."

"And maybe José and Manuel will learn the Lord's Prayer."

He had to smile at the thought of the parrots shouting prayers instead of insults. "Speaking of the dangerous duo, whatever possessed you to teach them some of those sayings? Didn't you realize you would be asking for trouble?"

"Most of what they know they learned from a previous owner. I've been cleaning up their act for the past eighteen months. I've been teaching them Shakespeare and some lines from old movies."

"Who owned them before you, Rodney Dangerfield?"

"No, some guy named Mad Dog who owned a theme bar down by the docks in Philadelphia."

"What was the theme, the scenic Amazon?"

"No, pirates. The place was a hangout for cutthroats and pirates until the board of health closed it down for numerous violations that Mad Dog refused to fix. Of course, it didn't help that he was in prison for killing two of his patrons for making fun of his peg leg."

He stared at her for a long time as she polished off the last of her food. She had to be joking. Didn't she? A pirate theme bar on the docks of Philadelphia. Hell, anything was possible nowadays. But a peg leg was pushing it a little too far. He had to remember what Maddie did for a living. She was an actress. A natural-born actress, if Glen was to be believed. "You're lying."

Maddie looked insulted, drank the rest of her milk, and grinned. "What gave me away, the bit about prison?"

"The peg leg was a tad much, Maddie." He shook his head. "Glen always said you were a fine actress. You didn't even crack a smile."

"Thanks, but when I don't have a script to follow I usually get too ambitious and push the story beyond belief." She slid off the stool and started to clean up their dishes.

He stood and immediately started to help. "So where did the little green monsters really come from?"

"When I lived in New York, I befriended a

nice old man who had the apartment next to mine. When he died eighteen months ago, I was informed that he had left me all his worldly possessions, which amounted to José and Manuel."

"You inherited them?"

"Not as exciting as getting them from the murdering owner of a pirate bar, but it's the truth."

He watched as Maddie finished wiping down the counter. Dinner was over and there really wasn't any reason for him to be hanging around. Expect for the vulnerability in her eyes. Those damn emerald-green eyes had turned all soft and uncertain. It was like she was watching her whole world crumble around her feet and there was nothing she could do about it. He had seen that look in her eyes only once before. Seventeen years ago . . .

Maddie had been fifteen and Georgia's best friend. He had been home from college for the summer and had tried avoiding her as much as possible. Her schoolgirl crush had been both painfully obvious and embarrassing. Maddie had been gawky then, pushing the five-foot eight-inch mark and boasting a mouth full of braces and a nose covered in freckles. Her hair had been a halo of fiery red curls.

One sunny afternoon by his parents' pool his luck ran out and he ended up face-to-face with his little sister's closest friend and in a very awkward position. Maddie made a pass at him. He considered various responses and decided the kindest thing he could do was to be cruel and end her infatuation quickly and forever. He figured a cold, clean break would kill whatever she thought she felt toward him, and she could then get on with her life and he could enjoy the remaining days of summer with his family. Afterward, seeing her look of devastation whenever he was around and knowing she was going away to boarding school that fall, leaving his sister without her best friend nearby, he had wondered if he had done the right thing.

Now, with the passage of the years, he knew he had handled the situation like a complete jerk. He hadn't been there for her when she needed someone to understand. He wasn't about to repeat that mistake.

He purposely walked toward her. Her eyes widened in surprise, but he didn't stop until he was inches from her. He reached up and cupped both of her cheeks. "Maddie, your father is going to be just fine."

Huge tears pooled in her eyes, and her voice cracked when she spoke. "That's what the doctors say."

"Believe them." His gaze slid down to her trembling mouth. Her mouth was on the generous side, and her nose and cheeks were still splashed with freckles. He could dry her tears, but what did one do with a quivering lip? He felt his own fingers tremble in response. "Glen's a fighter, Maddie. He's not going to let something as inconvenient as a mild stroke keep him down for long. You'll see, he'll be up and about in no time."

Maddie gave a delicate sniffle. "I know."

"Then why are you crying?"

Fresh tears gathered in her eyes, pushing huge drops over the rim and down her face to wet his fingertips. "I guess it's because I just realized my father isn't immortal." She sniffled again. "He could have died, Morgan." Her voice rose with each word. "I was up in Connecticut playing Lady Macbeth and my father could have died." By the time she completed the sentence her whole body was shaking.

Morgan pulled her into his arms and let her cry on his shoulder. He had done it for his sister; he could do it for Glen's daughter too. Her tears were soaking the front of his shirt, but he didn't care. He was too fascinated by the light fragrance of her shampoo. She smelled like peaches. He willed his hands not to pull her closer. This was Maddie, Glen's daughter. His hands slowly moved in a circular motion across her back as he glared at the far kitchen wall.

Her crying spell slowly ebbed, for which he was extremely thankful. Something was happening to him. Something he didn't want to think about or even admit. He was there to make sure she was all right and nothing more.

When she stepped back, he dropped his arms. "Better?"

"Embarrassed is more like it." She reached for a napkin and wiped her eyes. "I'm sorry about that. I usually don't make a habit of crying all over men's shirts."

"You've been under a lot of strain, Maddie. No apology is necessary." She still had the look of a confused little girl. His arms ached to hold her again, to make everything all right. He had to get the hell out of there before he did something really stupid, like give in to that urge. "Are you going to be all right now?"

"I'm fine, Morgan. Go on home and get some sleep. I'm sure we'll be running into each other at the hospital." She walked out of the kitchen and toward the front door. "Thanks again for checking on me and for being there when my father needed you."

He followed her out into the foyer and opened the front door. "Make sure you lock it behind me and keep it locked, Maddie." He gave her a quick glance and said, "See you," then headed down the brick path to the drive. Too many emotions were visible in her eyes. And every one of them struck a chord with him. Maybe that was the connection he was feeling with Maddie.

He had lost both his parents sixteen years ago and had only his sister left. Maddie had lost her mother twenty years ago and only had her father left. They both knew what suffering was and even the slightest brush in that direction could set off a flood of emotions.

He turned and watched as she closed the door. The connection with grief was part of what he was feeling. The other part was too absurd to even think about. He had wanted Maddie, as only a man could want a woman.

TWO

Maddie whipped off the dustcover and smiled at her latest find—a chrome and red Formica kitchen table and four chairs. It was straight out of the fifties and appeared to be in great shape. She pressed on one red vinyl seat and felt it crack and give beneath her fingers. Nothing a little reupholstering wouldn't fix. So far the small stone cottage, tucked away on a corner of her father's five acres of property, was perfect.

Well, nearly perfect. Most of the windows were stuck closed, the front door was warped so badly it refused to open, and the refrigerator was missing. Nothing that couldn't be fixed. The cedar-shake roof didn't leak, and all the electrical wiring had been replaced in the early sixties. The water was currently turned off, but that could be solved. All she had to do now was convince her father to let her move into the cottage.

Of course, it was going to take a couple of weeks before she was comfortable with the idea of her father staying by himself, now that he was home from the hospital. Her father's recovery had gone exactly as the doctors had predicted. She had brought him home from Lancaster General three days earlier and was relearning quite a few things about her father, things she had forgotten over the years and the miles. Glen Andrews was stubborn, liked things his way, and he hated being fussed over. The last trait he would have to change, because she was planning on fussing over him a lot. He just might accept it more if she did her fussing from two acres away instead of in the same house.

She glanced around the kitchen once again before stepping through the archway back into the living room. A good cleaning, a fresh coat of paint, and some bright, cheery curtains, and the cottage would be in better shape than most apartments she had lived in over the years.

"Maddie! Maddie, are you in there?"

She quickly turned toward the kitchen where the voice had come from. The voice that had haunted her dreams for years. What in the heck was Let-her-cry-all-over-his-shirt-and-make-a-fool-out-of-herself Morgan doing here? She stepped into the kitchen and looked at the man who had awakened her adolescent hormones when she had been only fifteen. Of course she had gotten over him, but still, it wouldn't take much to spark her infatuation again.

Wasn't it bad enough that she had run into him practically every night while her father had been in the hospital? Now he was invading her home. Home? She glanced around the kitchen with its nostalgic dinette set, dull wood floor, and thirty years of dust. Yes, home. The one-bedroom cottage would make a wonderful home. Near enough to her father that she could keep an eye on him and make sure he was following the doctors' orders, yet far enough away to give them both some privacy.

"Hello, Morgan. Are you lost?" She didn't like the way he just stepped into the cottage and looked around as if he owned it. Morgan had a habit of doing that. It didn't matter who he was with or where he was, he always seemed a bit above it all. He never said anything to give that impression, it was simply his presence. Morgan De Witt commanded attention just by being there. Of course, at six feet three inches tall, he was hard to miss. His height had never bothered her, though. Being five foot nine herself, she was only six inches shorter.

His eyes, however, did bother her. His eyes and his voice. Morgan had Humphrey Bogart's eyes and a voice to match. She loved Humphrey Bogart and just about every picture he had made.

Morgan's deep brown eyes reflected his soul and made any woman within gazing distance want to fall right into them. He seemed to see everything that went on around him, yet he distanced himself from it all. He always struck her as rather cynical and hard, yet with a touch of sadness about him, occasionally glimpsed in those "Casablanca" eyes.

Rumor had it that there had been a love affair that had gone wrong, just like Bogey's Rick Blaine in *Casablanca*. She didn't hold much stock in rumors, but it would explain the impregnable wall that seemed to surround him. She had noticed a few cracks in that wall, especially where her father was concerned. Morgan couldn't have been more devoted to her father if he were his son. Did that make him a kind of big brother to her?

She studied him as he surveyed the kitchen. His face was too masculine to be classed as "pretty boy" handsome. His jaw was square and showed a five o'clock shadow, even though it was barely two in the afternoon. His conservatively cut brown hair was so dark it was nearly black. Lines fanned out from the corners of his eyes and bracketed his stern, unsmiling mouth. The bridge of his nose had a slight bump, where to the unknowing eye it would appear he had been on the receiving end of a powerful fist. She knew better. At sixteen he had been on the receiving end of a misused ice hockey stick.

The overall impression that Morgan conveyed was one of hard times and violence. It was a totally false impression, and Maddie saw the evidence of that in his mouth. Though his upper lip was thin and unyielding, his lower lip had a seductive fullness to it that hinted at his hidden softness and made her wonder what it would be like to be kissed by him.

Over a week ago, when he had held her in her father's kitchen while she cried her eyes out, he hadn't felt like a big brother. He had felt like a rock, a friend, and something more. Something she didn't want to examine too closely.

His scrutiny of the dusty, musty-smelling kitchen was getting on her nerves. "Morgan, did you want something?"

He closed the door of the cabinet he had been looking in. "Your father sent me to find you." He glanced through the archway into the living room. "He thought you were out walking in the gardens."

"Is something wrong?" When she'd left her father's house a half hour ago, he had been with the physical therapist. Her father didn't like an audience during his sessions, so she had taken the cottage key from the hook in the kitchen and headed out the back door.

"No, your father's fine. He had just finished up with the therapist and was heading for the shower when I arrived."

"Did he say why he wanted me?" Was she supposed to act as hostess to Morgan while her father freshened up?

"Well, actually, he wants us both."

"Both?"

"Glen called me this morning and asked me to stop over. He said there was something he needed to discuss with us."

"What could he possibly want to talk to both of us about?" As far as she knew the only common ground Morgan and she had was her father. That didn't explain why her father had asked Morgan over.

"I can't rightly say." Morgan stepped into the living room. "I never knew your father had a bungalow back here."

"It was built in the thirties as a home for a married couple who worked for my grandparents. After they passed away it stood empty for years until my father had it fixed up as a guesthouse for some of my mother's friends who visited quite often when they were first married. After I was born it was closed up and the guests stayed up at the main house."

She watched as Morgan studied a lamp made from a hunk of driftwood. She had seen a lamp almost identical to it in one of those trendy nostalgia stores. She could have purchased three brand-new lamps for what they had wanted for that old one. "The cottage is in great shape except for a few minor things that can be easily repaired."

"Plan on reopening it as a guesthouse?"

"No." She glanced out the huge living room window to the gardens beyond. "I plan on moving into it as soon as I feel my father will be fine alone in the house."

Morgan walked down the small hallway, giving the tiny bathroom a curious glance before stepping into the bedroom. "Glen's tossing you and your uncivil talking pets out?"

Maddie frowned as she stood in the bedroom doorway watching him. There was something unnerving about Morgan standing in the room where she planned on sleeping in a very short time. The bedroom set was the bleached-white wood with bulky chrome handles that had been so popular back in the fifties. She thought the room had a certain charm. Of course, the charm was now buried beneath dirt, rotted curtains, and the pile of dustcovers she had pulled off the furniture. "José and Manuel are not uncivil. In fact, they are extremely friendly and my father finds them . . ." She wasn't really sure what her father thought of the parrots. At first he had considered them amusing, but being called "hamster brain" every time he walked into the living room was wearing thin. Mighty thin. ". . . entertaining." She nodded as she spoke the word. "He finds them very entertaining."

Morgan made a choking sound, that sounded suspiciously like a chuckle. "I'm sure he does."

"He's especially fond of Manuel."

"I'd say that if he hasn't stuffed and roasted the pair by now, he is indeed fond of the mouthy duo."

"Stop threatening my birds."

"I didn't threaten them." Morgan seemed amused by the idea. "I merely stated the facts. There are only two reasons those birds are still in Glen's home. Either for some unknown masochistic reason he actually likes them, or he's tolerating them because of their owner."

She didn't like the way that sounded. If they were that much of an inconvenience to her father, surely he would have said something. It wasn't as if he were allergic to cats and she had brought two of them into his house. José and Manuel were just cute little birds who happened to talk a bit. "As soon as I move in here, he won't have to tolerate them at all." She left the bedroom and walked through the living room toward the kitchen.

"So your father was speaking the truth when he said you were home for good."

"I haven't ever known my father not to speak the truth." She headed for the open kitchen door. "I already told you I was back to stay. Didn't you believe me?"

"I didn't mean that how it sounded, Maddie. I know you told me, but I figured it was the stress talking." He followed her out the door.

She closed the door behind them, but didn't lock it. She was going to come back later in the afternoon and make a list of repairs. "What did you expect? That I would head back to Connecticut as soon as he was out of danger and get on with my life?"

Morgan shrugged. "Well, it is your life."

"Yes, it is." She had had two discussions so far with her father about moving back to Lancaster. At first he had argued and told her she would change her mind. It had taken a while, but eventually he had understood that she meant it. She was staying. "Speaking of it being my life, I would like you not to mention the cottage to my father."

"He doesn't know you're moving into it?"

They headed for the main house, following a twisting garden path. "I haven't asked him yet." The late summer sun and fresh air felt wonderful after being in the stuffy cottage. The gardens were in full bloom and the fragrance was sweet enough to make a perfume manufacturer cry. Her father's one joy in life was gardening.

Glen Andrews spent most of his spare time digging in the soil, pruning, planting, and just soaking up the fresh country air. Nothing gave her father more pleasure than his gardens. It had been one of his biggest concerns while lying in the hospital bed—who was going to take care of his precious plants? Maddie had assured him she wouldn't so much as touch a leaf. It was a sad, cruel joke that Glen Andrews's daughter had been born with a notorious brown thumb. If she touched it, it would die.

She glanced at Morgan, who was dressed in casual khaki pants and a dark blue and khaki print polo shirt. He looked like he was thinking about something besides the gorgeous array of flowers bordering the path they were walking down. He didn't even notice the half-dozen butterflies fluttering around them. "Are you sure you don't know what my father wants to talk to us about?"

"I have a hunch."

She stopped in the middle of the path, frowning at him. "What's your hunch?" Whatever his suspicion was, he didn't look too happy about it.

"I might be wrong." Morgan walked around the marble fountain of a young girl pouring water from an urn and headed for the steps leading up to the slate terrace. "Why don't we wait and be surprised."

"I hate surprises." She climbed the two steps and opened the French doors. He knew what this was about and he didn't want to tell her.

He followed her into the house and softly closed the doors behind them. "I'll have to remember that."

She turned and faced him for a moment. His eyes held her enthralled. He seemed to be committing that small tidbit of information to his memory. Why would it matter one way or the other if Morgan knew how much she hated being surprised? The whole idea was absurd. "You do that."

She turned and headed for the hallway and her father's study. Morgan was directly behind her and the door was open. She stepped into the study and walked straight to her father, who was sitting at his desk. She kissed him on his cheek, noting the healthy glow the strenuous therapy session had brought to his face. "How did the workout go today?"

The day before, she had driven him to the hospital for his session. For the next several weeks the sessions would be alternated between the hospital and home. She could see an improvement already since he had left the hospital. The stroke had affected his left side. He had to use a walker, and it was still difficult for him to get up and down and to gain his balance. He had regained much of his mobility in his left arm, but not all. Still, anyone seeing him sitting there behind his desk would never guess he'd had a stroke, if it weren't for his face. The left corner of his mouth and the area around his eye were still slack. His speech was still slightly slurred, but it, too, was improving daily.

Glen groaned in response to her question. "That woman had to have worked in a dungeon torturing prisoners in a previous life."

She chuckled. "I didn't think you believed in previous lives, Dad."

"I didn't until I met her. The rack would have been more merciful."

"But you're getting better. She must be doing something right."

"That's the only reason I'm allowing her to come back." Glen aimed a half smile at Morgan. "Thanks for finding her for me."

"No problem," Morgan said.

Glen waved to the two comfortable armchairs in front of his desk. "Would you both please sit down for a moment."

Maddie frowned, but walked around to the front of the desk and sat. Whatever her father wanted to discuss had to be important. Major discussions always took place in her father's study with her sitting across the desk from him. She felt Morgan's gaze linger a tad too long on her legs, and wondered if she shouldn't have changed into a skirt or a pair of pants. The shorts and T-shirt she had pulled on that morning seemed inappropriate for this discussion. "What's so important, Dad, that you had to send Morgan out after me?"

Glen's gaze darted back and forth between the two of them, as if he were trying to figure out something important. "I'm not sure where to begin, Maddie, so please bear with me."

Her father studied the leather-bound folder lying on his desk for a long time. "Andrews Quarries has been in the family for generations, and it's very important to me. I know the quarry business never interested you, Maddie, but there's something you should be aware of." He smiled at her. "Lance Cummings stopped by last night at my request. You know Lance is my attorney as well as a friend. When we came in here to talk shop, I signed papers to give you power of attorney and the title of President of Andrews Quarries in case anything should happen to me."

She couldn't contain her gasp of dismay.

Stunned by his announcement, she stood up and quickly walked to the window overlooking the gardens. Of all the things she regretted in life, not being the son her father wanted had to top the list. Maybe being born a son instead of a daughter wasn't the correct way of looking at it. Her father wanted someone, be it a son or a daughter, to leave his business to. He wanted Andrews Quarries to continue to thrive long after he had departed from this earth. In college she had tried to major in business, only to nearly flunk out her first year at N.Y.U. It had taken her father to show her the error of her ways. He had said he only wanted her happiness, not an heir to the business, and she had believed him.

Now, he had gone and made her the president of Andrews Quarries when she knew absolutely nothing about stones and rocks. Heck, she didn't even appreciate precious gemstones. She much preferred the sparkling fake baubles of the theater.

"Now, Maddie, hear me out," continued Glen as she turned around and faced him. "I had a lot of time on my hands lying in that hospital bed. In fact, I probably had too much time." He cleared his throat and toyed with the edges of the leather folder. "I realized a long time ago, Maddie, that the footsteps you were to follow in weren't mine, but your mother's. Nothing has given me greater joy than to watch you follow the path of your dreams."

She refused to allow the tears pooling in the

corners of her eyes to spill over. They would only upset her father and embarrass her in front of Morgan. Again. Why Morgan had been invited to this personal family rehashing of business was still a mystery, but she was willing to bet she wouldn't like the reason when she found out. "So why would you give me power of attorney to a business I know nothing about? Aren't you worried that with a few misguided strokes of a pen I could wipe out your entire life's work?"

Her father smiled. "Not really." He nodded toward Morgan. "During a couple of Morgan's visits to the hospital we talked about business. Much, I'm sure, to Morgan's dismay, I called in a favor. Sixteen years ago when his parents died, he was left a floundering asphalt business he knew next to nothing about. I offered my friendship, my services, and my advice whenever he thought he could use them."

"I called on your father quite a lot in the beginning, Maddie," Morgan offered as an explanation. "Glen pointed me in the right direction on more than one occasion. I owe him more than I could ever repay."

"Nonsense, Morgan. I might have hinted at the directions, but all the credit for the success of the business is yours. Your father and mother would have been extremely proud of you." Glen turned his attention back to her. "Just as your mother would have been, and I most assuredly am proud of you, Maddie. Morgan has agreed to act as your adviser should anything happen to me."

She didn't want to think about anything happening to her father or Morgan advising her about business. "What about Carl Roberts? He ran the business just fine while you were in the hospital."

"Carl's a good man, Maddie. He's the perfect second-in-command. For the past couple of weeks, the business ran as smoothly as ever. Carl just lacks the fortitude or experience to see the future. Andrews Quarries wouldn't last two years with Carl at the helm."

"So why didn't you get Morgan to agree to advise Carl? Why bring me into this at all?" She could understand her father planning for any future emergencies, especially after the scare he had had, but why name her president?

"As medieval as it sounds, I don't want the business to pass out of the Andrews family. I want my flesh and blood to inherit the quarries."

She felt as if she had just downed a quart of Chunky Monkey ice cream and had developed the biggest ice-cream headache she'd ever experienced. Her father wanted an Andrews at the helm of the business after all. Maybe his stroke wasn't as mild as the doctors had assured her it had been. She took a couple of steps toward him and smiled wryly. "Dad, do you have a couple, or even one, illegitimate kids that I don't know about?"

"Nope. You're my only offspring, sweet Maddie with the emerald-green eyes."

She refused to be swayed by the loving tone of her father's voice. When she was little, he used to pull her onto his lap and sing about a wee Irish lass named Sweet Maddie who had emerald-green eyes and a line of princes willing to battle a fire-breathing dragon to win her fair hand. It had been a great confidence builder when she was small, but at thirty-two it was going to take more than a childhood memory to soften her up. "Excuse me if I seem a little confused. You are willing to allow me to follow my chosen path and not put in an apprenticeship to head the quarry business, right?"

"That's correct, my dear. I would never force you to do anything you didn't want to do."

Her raging headache went from migraine to possibly terminal. Her father wasn't making any sense. Morgan's presence in the room ceased to be important. She had a more pressing problem to deal with, namely her father's sanity. "Then how do you expect a flesh-and-blood Andrews to inherit the quarries?"

Glen's grin would have stretched from ear to ear if it hadn't been for the effects of the stroke on his left side. "I have that all figured out, Maddie. It's so simple, I don't know why I never thought of it before."

"Thought of what?"

"Grandchildren."

At that one word, she felt a familiar, painful ache, the one that happened every time she pictured her father bouncing a grandchild on his knee. She willed the ache to lessen and took a deep breath. "Dad, in case you haven't noticed, you don't have any grandchildren."

"Not yet, but I'm sure I will one day." Glen gave Morgan a conspiring wink. "You've turned into one fine woman, Maddie. Just like your mother."

This time the ache didn't just grip her heart, it twisted its way around it and started to strangle it. "So you've been telling me for the past twenty years. What does that have to do with grandchildren?" She really didn't want to continue this conversation. She knew where it was going to end: in heartbreak, hers. She had been trained to act, and act she would. Her father wasn't going to see how much the subject of children, children she would never have, upset her.

"Carolyn wanted children more than anything in the world," her father said. "You're the same, Maddie. You should have a houseful of little tykes. One out of the bunch, I'm sure, will inherit some of my blood and want to run the quarries."

Her mother had wanted a houseful of children, but the strain of her first pregnancy had weakened her heart to the point where it was too dangerous to add another little lad or lassie to the Andrews household. For twenty years Maddie had been carrying around the guilt of being the cause of her mother's heart condition, and eventually her death. She wasn't about to pass that heavy burden of guilt on to her own child. "Dad, you seem to be forgetting something."

"What's that?"

"I'm not married." Nor did she have any intention of getting married. Surely her father wouldn't want her to have a bunch of kids out of wedlock just so he'd have someone to pass the business on to.

Glen's gaze traveled the length of her body and back up again. He frowned. "Morgan, I'll be the first one to admit that I'm prejudiced on the subject of my daughter, so I want you to answer truthfully. Can you see one thing wrong with her? She should have a line of men taking numbers at the front door just to get a date with her. I don't understand it. What's wrong with men nowadays?"

She no longer felt the ache in her heart. The acute embarrassment turning her face a brilliant red was going to kill her. "Father!"

Morgan chuckled and shook his head. "It's the hair that's keeping them away."

She rounded on Morgan and snapped, "What's wrong with my hair?"

"It's the color, Maddie. Red-haired women are nothing but trouble." Morgan shrugged and winked at Glen. "Ask any American male. He'll tell you that redheads are notorious for their temper."

Glen laughed. "You wouldn't let a little thing like a temper scare you off, would you, Morgan?"

Morgan's grin grew and he seemed to be enjoying himself immensely. "That, my friend, would depend entirely on the woman."

A queasy feeling landed like a cement block in the pit of her stomach. Was her father trying to play matchmaker with Morgan and her? Oh, saints preserve them all! Who would have dreamed that a gorgeous day like today could have turned out so awful? She turned on her father. "Dad, why was Morgan invited to participate in this ridiculous discussion?" Morgan obviously already knew about his role in the quarries.

Glen's mirth faded as he studied his daughter's face. He seemed to read her mind. "Now, Maddie, it isn't what you're thinking."

"Isn't it?" She couldn't think of one other reason why Morgan had been privy to this humiliation. Her father wanted her to pair up with Morgan so she could start producing little De Witt–Andrews heirs. The combining of De Witt Asphalt and Andrews Quarries wouldn't be just a major business merger, it would be phenomenal.

"No, it isn't," Glen said. "I might want a grandchild very much, but I'm not witless enough to start tossing prospective sons-in-law at you. When you marry, it should be for one reason and one reason only: love."

"Well, thank you for that at least." She still wasn't planning on getting married, but it was nice to know her father wanted her to marry for love and not just to produce an heir. She refused to look at Morgan to see how he was reacting to this entire episode.

"I invited Morgan here because I still need his help. Even if you have a baby within a year, it would be another twenty-two years or more before the child could assume the helm. I'm approaching retirement age now, so I'm having a hard time seeing me run the quarries that far into the future."

"You want Morgan to run the quarries for you?" It made perfect sense to her. There wasn't a man better qualified for the job.

"Something like that." Glen picked up a silver-plated pen from his desk and tapped it against the folder. "I wanted you to know which direction I was planning on taking the quarries. Morgan and I can work out the business end of the agreement, if we can reach one."

She got the impression her father had just called an end to the meeting. Her presence was no longer required. Her job was to find a suitable husband and start knocking out those heirs. It was a real shame she wouldn't be complying. "I'll leave you two alone to plan your strategies." She walked around the desk and placed a kiss on her father's cheek. "Don't keep at it too long. I want you to lie down and get some rest this afternoon."

Her father returned her kiss with one of his own. "Stop worrying about me. I'm not tired."

She gave Morgan a slight nod without meeting his gaze. "Good-bye, Morgan."

Here's Lookin' at You

She walked to the door and glanced back at her father. He looked so commanding and powerful sitting behind his desk. It never ceased to amaze her how fragile the human body could be. "Dad, would you do me one favor while you're figuring out the future of the quarries?"

"Name it."

"Make an alternative plan in case there aren't any grandchildren." She couldn't bear to see his look of sadness, so she stepped out into the hall and softly closed the door behind her.

The tears she had been so gallantly holding back overflowed and streamed down her cheeks like twin rivers as she made her way onto the back terrace. She swiped at the tears as she passed the fountain and headed in the direction of the rose arbor. She'd learned the twisted paths as a child and could maneuver the turns blindfolded. With the tears blurring her vision she hurried on, farther into the gardens. She needed to reach the cottage. In the lonely shadows of the cottage, no one would see her pain.

THREE

Maddie leaned back in the soft leather chair and closed her eyes. She might as well have been reading gibberish for the last two hours for all she understood about running a quarry. You take big rocks and break them into little rocks. Sounded like a no-brainer to her, except she knew how dangerous the business could be. Her father's company preferred to use explosives to break off huge masses of rock from their place in the earth. In any business where explosives were used, nothing was a no-brainer.

If she was going to be honest with herself, she would have to admit she had understood a lot more than she wanted to. The simple plain truth was quarries, rocks, and the process of making big rocks into little rocks bored the hell out of her. She would rather study to become a dental hygienist and scrape people's teeth all day than sit behind a desk and push papers at Andrews Quarries.

But she loved her father beyond measure, and therein lay the problem.

He had named her president in the event something should happen to him. She prayed daily that nothing would happen to him, but she knew she had to be reasonable about both retirement and her father's mortality. He was not going to be able to run Andrews Quarries for eternity. If she refused to do as he asked, it would be like telling him his life's work was all for nothing. She couldn't do that to him. She respected her father's chosen career path. She just didn't want to follow it.

When she'd brought her father to work that morning, she had agreed to spend some time acquainting herself with the business while he put in a few hours behind his desk. They were then going to have a nice lunch at the country club, then she was taking him for his afternoon therapy session at the hospital. She had been so pleased that her father showed some interest in getting out of the house and visiting the club and his friends that she would have probably agreed to just about anything. Her father's recovery had been progressing so well, he was ahead of schedule, but he was still self-conscious of his slight limp and the weakness in his left arm.

"Taking a nap?" her father asked. "Or were you so bored you fell asleep?"

She opened her eyes and smiled at her father, standing in the doorway to the office he had let her use. "I was trying to let it all sink in, Dad. I think better with my eyes closed."

Glen stepped into the office. "You used to try to play the piano the same way." He chuckled. "Your mother and I used to sit there in amazement as you closed your eyes and swore you could see the notes in your mind." He shook his head. "You never did learn to play the piano."

"Hey, I can do a mean 'Chopsticks' and the easy part of the 'Heart and Soul' duet." She had to laugh along with her father. Playing an instrument wasn't her forte. She could hold a decent note and belt out a song without having an audience throw rotten vegetables at the stage. As for her piano playing, she was afraid her parents had wasted quite a bit of money on lessons. Even the flute that she had begged her parents to buy so she could be in the fifth-grade band had never made it to the sixth grade.

"Your mother always claimed you inherited your musical ability from me."

"Lord, I hope not, Dad. I've heard you singing in the shower and it isn't an experience I would care to repeat." On the other hand, Maddie knew her mother had loved to play the piano. On their first wedding anniversary her father had given her mother a baby grand. The beautiful piano that her mother had so loved was still in the back room that overlooked the gardens. It had been silent for the past twenty years.

"You have your mother's voice, Maddie. There's no mistake about that. It would take more than my nonexistent musical gene to screw it up. Carolyn sang like an angel."

Her father's sad little smile pulled at her heart. After all these years, he still loved her. Twelve years of knowing his wife had a bad heart hadn't been enough to prepare him for her death. The day they buried her mother was the day her father sank so far into his whiskey bottle, it had taken him more than two years to climb back out.

She had only been twelve years old when she'd lost her mother to the cold ground and her father to the whiskey. Her father drank to kill the pain and shut out the world, but she hadn't had that option. She had been devastated and confused by her father's lack of interest in her and even his own life. She had started hiding from her father and his pain and had practically lived at Georgia De Witt's house. Georgia's parents understood her pain and had always welcomed her with open arms. She had found a substitute family for the one she lost. It wasn't surprising she'd developed a crush on Morgan. Even after her father had shaken off his depression and woke up to the fact he still had a daughter, he never regained his spark for life. Glen Andrews was a changed man, and with that he changed his daughter.

She had sworn she would never get married

and chance putting her spouse or herself through such total devastation. Love had the power to destroy. It was a powerful lesson for a young girl to learn. Her father hadn't been strong enough to work through his own grief, let alone help her through hers. She didn't blame her father or think anything less of him. She loved him just as much today as she had when she was twelve, or even when she was three. Glen Andrews was and always would be her father and the only man capable of claiming part of her heart.

Just because she loved him, though, didn't mean she would ever love another. Her father's wish of seeing her married and blessing him with grandchildren would never become a reality. The risk was too great, the lesson had been too harsh.

She gave her father a sad smile of her own. "Mom could have sung like a cat caught in barbed wire and you would have thought it was an angel, Dad."

"True, but she did have a lovely voice." His smile didn't seem so sad any longer. "When you were four you used to climb up on the piano bench next to her and pound on the keys and try to sing songs you didn't know the words to. Your mother used to make up silly verses and the both of you would laugh and make such a game out of it."

"You still miss her, don't you?"

Glen nodded. "Every day, Maddie. Every

day." He glanced at the folders sitting in front of her. "Are you ready to leave?"

She looked at her watch. "It's only eleven o'clock. What's the hurry?"

"I told Morgan we'd stop by his place to pick him up for lunch."

"Morgan? Why is Morgan coming to lunch with us?" First she had cried all over his shirt, then her father had practically thrown her at him in an attempt to gain some grandchildren. Now Morgan was invading their lunch.

"I need to go over a few things with him." Glen picked up the folders. "Since you'll only let me work a couple of hours a day, I'm having a hard time squeezing everything in. I figured I could kill two birds with one lunch. Besides, you should try to pay attention to our conversation. You might learn a thing or two about the business." He winked at her. "But do try not to fall asleep over your meal."

She held back her groan as Glen walked out of the office with the folders she had been going through. It looked like her father was definitely on the road to a full recovery and was gaining back control of his life. That meant her job of "mothering" him was going to get twice as difficult.

Maddie glanced around the elegant reception area of De Witt Asphalt and was impressed. She hadn't expected some fly-by-night operation where they'd laid asphalt on the floor to display it to potential customers, but she hadn't been expecting this either. Plush, dark green carpet cushioned their feet, the walls were painted a light green, and warmly polished wood was everywhere. Whoever had decorated the area had brought in the feel of the surrounding country. Lancaster County was the heart of Pennsylvania Dutch country, and Morgan's offices reflected that heart. A hand-stitched Amish quilt hung on one wall, while on the others were gorgeous paintings and prints of the Amish way of life. No plaques or framed certificates cluttered the wall. A ten-foot potted tree reached for the skylights that brightened the entire area.

The fashionably dressed receptionist replaced the phone she had just been talking into. "Angela says I'm to send you both back. Mr. De Witt is tied up in a meeting, but she assured me it will be breaking up soon."

Glen smiled. "Thanks, Peg."

"Anytime, Mr. Andrews." Peg gave Glen a friendly smile. "I'm so glad to see you're up and about. We were all quite concerned for you, Mr. Andrews, when Mr. De Witt told us about your illness."

"It would take more than a simple stroke to hold me down. And how many times must I tell you to call me Glen, Peg?"

"Mr. De Witt likes a formal office."

Glen chuckled. "Any time you want to work

for a more relaxed company, Peg, you give me a call."

Peg only shook her head and smiled. "You remember where Mr. De Witt's offices are, don't you?"

"I should. I'm the first one Morgan showed the blueprints to after he picked them up from the architect."

Glen started down the hall to the left. Maddie pulled her attention from a particularly exquisite painting of an Amish boy leading a baby calf through a meadow of tall grass and wildflowers, and followed her father.

The offices they passed were filled with activity. Telephones rang, computers printed, and serious, low-toned voices sounded everywhere. The only office complex she knew well was her father's. The main offices for Andrews Quarries were just as busy, but they seemed to have a more friendly and relaxed atmosphere than here. Morgan obviously ran one very tight ship.

"Glen, you old son of a gun, how are you feeling?"

Maddie watched as her father was greeted by a man with a booming voice and a body to match. The six-and-a-half-foot tall giant seemed to take up the entire hallway.

"Ben, good to see you," said Glen as he shook the giant's hand. "Thanks for the bouquet of balloons and the get-well wishes." Glen puffed out his chest and thumped it. "As you can see, they worked."

Ben grinned. "Glad to see it. The balloons were the wife's idea. She said we couldn't very well send you flowers, considering your hobby. I suggested a box of cigars, but she said she'd have my head on a platter if I dared." Ben shook his head, looking baffled. "Damned if I know what to send a man in the hospital."

"The balloons were perfect. They brightened up the room and when I left, Maddie took them down to the pediatric ward for the little ones." Glen motioned her forward. "Ben, I would like you to meet my daughter, Maddie."

"Hello, Maddie." Ben reached out and shook her hand. "Your father does nothing but brag about you."

"Hello, Ben. Sorry if my father bored you."

Glen and Ben both chuckled. "Maddie," Glen said, "why don't you go to Morgan's office and see if he's ready. I have a few things I want to run by Ben while I'm here."

"You're supposed to be taking it easy, Dad, and I don't know where Morgan's office is."

"Ben won't let me do anything strenuous. I'll be sitting in a chair, Maddie, not shoveling asphalt." Glen looked at Ben and rolled his eyes, as if to say *Daughters!* "Morgan's office is straight ahead. His door will be guarded by the sainted patron of composure named Angela."

She glanced down the hall, but all she could

see were a set of double doors, some chairs off to the side, a few towering plants, and sunshine. Angela's desk was out of view. She shook her head as her father practically pushed Ben back into his office. Her father's rudeness could be explained by one of two things. Ben was either the man in charge of purchasing all the stone and gravel needed at De Witt Asphalt, or her father was up to his matchmaking tricks.

The other day in his study hadn't been a fluke. Glen had been trying his hand at matchmaking. For the past week all she had heard were sly little questions slipped into unrelated conversations. *"What do you think of Morgan?" "Did Morgan make sure you were all settled in the night you arrived?" "Manuel didn't call Morgan hamster brain or anything insulting, did he?"* Morgan had become a topic of great interest to her father.

She stepped into the well-lit area and smiled at the woman sitting behind a desk. She appeared to be around forty years old and looked like the epitome of the professional woman. Her fingers were flying over the keyboard of her computer, but she looked up as Maddie approached her desk.

"You must be Madeline Andrews," the woman said. "I'm Angela Weaver, Mr. De Witt's secretary." Angela glanced around. "Where's Mr. Andrews?"

"He's in with Ben. He asked me to see if Morgan's ready." It had been on the tip of her tongue to call Morgan Mr. De Witt, but she couldn't do it. She had known Morgan since she was a little girl and he had been just a skinny kid who yelled at her and Georgia if they went into his room.

"I'm sure the meeting is just about over."

Even as Angela spoke, the double doors swung inward and a half-dozen men walked out of Morgan's office. By the looks on some of their faces, Maddie wasn't sure if the meeting had been a success or not.

"Good," Angela said, "it's over. Why don't you go ahead in? Mr. De Witt is expecting you."

"Thank you." Maddie glanced into the office and only saw Morgan sitting at his desk with his back toward the room. He was staring out the huge plate-glass window behind his desk. She stepped into the room and was about to call his name when she noticed the phone held to his ear.

"And I'm telling you it can't be done for that price," he was saying. "They're underpricing by tens of thousands of dollars because they want to lose money and declare bankruptcy. Then the state will have to step in and bail them out. The state will not only be getting half-assed workmanship that will have no guarantee because the company will be out of business, but the state will be footing the bill for it too."

Maddie took only a quick look around the spacious office before focusing her attention on Morgan. He was upset and angry about something. Though she could only hear his side of the conversation, she guessed whomever he was talking to was pretty important.

After a lengthy pause, he went on. "Of course I know they're going to say it's sour grapes on my part because De Witt's didn't get the contract. So give the contract to one of my other competitors or to the next lowest bidder. Hell, put bids out again for the job. I don't care. My only concern is the way the state is being ripped off, which means taxpayers are being ripped off.

"Hell, I'm of half a mind to start lobbying for reform on the bidding practices of this state. Cheapest is not always the best."

Morgan ran his fingers through his hair as the other person spoke, then he slumped farther down in his chair. "It happened two years ago with the Ace Asphalt Company. The state only got to withhold its final payment, and the road was a total disaster. The state can't afford to hire the number of inspectors needed for every road being repaired or built, and Ace slipped through the proverbial cracks. The state ended up paying triple what the last payment would have been in order to repair and complete the road. The state also got the privilege of bailing Ace out in bankruptcy court and Ace's creditors got a lousy twenty cents on the dollar. Somewhere, Noah, this has got to end."

Maddie's eyebrows rose in surprise. Morgan was talking about lobbying for reform, stopping companies from ripping off the state and performing shoddy work. He seemed so disgusted by the whole thing, yet so determined to do something.

"Well, of course, Noah, that's all I wanted you to do, to look into it. Give us an even and fair playing field, not only for my company, but for the other honest, hardworking guys out there trying to make a living. There's a lot of grumbling going on, Noah, and not only in the asphalt industry. I'm afraid bidding reform isn't too far off in the future."

Maddie softly walked closer to his desk and stopped by a leather chair directly in front of it. She could see Morgan's reflection in the glass. He looked determined, not angry. Morgan De Witt would be a force to reckon with on the business front.

His eyes widened with recognition as his reflected gaze collided with hers. "It's been good talking to you, Noah. You too. 'Bye." Morgan swung his chair around and hung up the phone. "Hello, Maddie. I didn't hear you come in."

"Angela said you were expecting me."

"I was." He glanced behind her. "Where's your father?"

"He met someone named Ben and they went into his office. I was to see if you're ready yet." Now that he was facing her, she could see that Morgan looked devastatingly handsome in his deep gray suit, white shirt, and conservative striped tie. Talk about a power suit. She nodded to the phone. "Problem?"

"Nothing that can't be dealt with."

"Who were you talking to?"

"Noah Wenger."

"*Senator* Noah Wenger?"

"Yes." Morgan stood up and straightened the sleeve of his suit. "Are you ready to go or would you like a quick tour of the facilities?"

She shook her head in awe. He had been talking to State Senator Noah Wenger! No wonder her father idolized the business ground Morgan walked on. The man talked to state senators with great familiarity and even hinted at lobbying for reform on something as entrenched as the state's bidding laws. Morgan could step into her father's shoes at Andrews Quarries tomorrow without even missing a beat. Her father had chosen well. It was a real shame fate had not seen fit to bless her father with a son like Morgan. Instead he had gotten a daughter who couldn't play the piano and preferred the smell of greasepaint over Chanel No. 5.

"I'll take you up on the tour some other time," she said. "Right now I think we should drag my father out of Ben's office. He's supposed to be taking it easy. He put in three and a half hours at work this morning."

Morgan stepped around the desk and took her arm to lead her from the office. "Ben won't overtax your father. Knowing Ben, they're probably discussing what killed his wife's roses this summer."

She allowed Morgan to keep his light grip on her. Today was the first time she had actually seen him in his element. It was a real eye-opener. The mahogany desk, the efficient staff, the huge office, even the senator on the phone suited him. He wasn't the easygoing college student she remembered from her youth. Morgan had grown up into one successful and powerful man.

Maddie felt like she was eating lunch in a fishbowl. Everyone around them kept staring at their table. At first she'd thought they were all looking at her father, curious as to the progress he had made. But after a few of his friends stopped by the table, wishing him well and expressing their happiness at seeing him out and about, she began to realize they were staring at her. The prodigal daughter had returned.

So far the main conversation at their table had been between Morgan and her father, centering mostly on business. She nodded politely, murmured a few words when appropriate, but mostly she pushed her stuffed flounder around her plate and willed herself not to do anything stupid, like stand up on the middle of their table and start raving like Katharina in *The Taming of the Shrew*.

"Maddie?"

She blinked and looked at her father as he spoke her name for the second time. "I'm sorry, Dad, did you say something?"

"I asked if you would excuse me for a moment. Brenda Benson is across the room eating with one of her sons. I wanted to stop by and say hello."

Maddie looked across the room at Brenda, her mind immediately churning with a dozen thoughts. Brenda had been a constant visitor at the hospital and at the house since her father's stroke. Was it possible there was something more than friendship between her father and the lovely widow? "Go ahead, Dad. I'm sure Morgan and I can keep each other company."

Glen pushed his chair back and left.

Morgan chuckled. "I guess he was in a hurry. He didn't even wait for dessert."

She shook her head, watching as her father wove his way around tables. "I have a feeling there's more to their friendship than he's telling me." Glen pulled a chair over to Brenda's table and sat down. She hadn't seen him smile like that in ages.

"Brenda's a very nice lady, Maddie. I think they'll be good for each other."

"You won't get any argument from me." She turned back around and took a sip of her iced tea. "How long has it been going on?" Her father had been building a relationship with a wonderful woman while she had been living in Connecticut, playing Lady Macbeth and plotting against King Duncan. She thought it was sweet, but wondered why her father hadn't told her about Brenda.

"I can't rightly say, Maddie. I've seen them

together occasionally, but never considered it was romantic." Morgan placed his napkin beside his plate. "Concerned?"

"No. My father's a grown man. I was just curious as to what all I might have missed while living so far away."

"Nothing much. The place is the same as it's always been. A little more populated, but basically the same. Nothing much changes around here."

She couldn't agree there. Morgan had changed. Physically he had filled out quite nicely over the years. Under his expensive suit his shoulders looked broad enough to carry the world. His face had the lines and the character of a man who knew that weight, and knew it intimately. The past seventeen years hadn't been easy on Morgan. "I saw in the paper that Georgia got married on Saturday."

"It was a small private ceremony with mainly just family. Georgia's very much in love with her husband."

"I would hope so. Father tells me Levi Horst is the carpenter who's working on her newest antique shop."

"True. They only met a couple of months ago. Georgia says it was love at first sight. All I know is my sister is a happily married woman now, with a sixteen-year-old stepson."

The expression on his face would have been comical if it wasn't so touching. It was a cross between relief and total bafflement. She suspected many parents wore that same expression a week after one of their children married. Morgan had taken care of Georgia since she was sixteen. In a way he was part older brother and part father. "Don't you believe in love at first sight, or is it the fact that you're now an uncle that upsets you?"

"The whole thing just happened so fast, that's all. One day she's discussing a business trip she had taken to West Virginia and the next she's trying on wedding gowns."

"I hear it happens like that sometimes." She couldn't imagine it herself, but she had heard stories. "Georgia's one smart woman. I'm sure she knows exactly what she's doing."

"I never thought she didn't." Morgan's gaze narrowed on her for an instant. It seemed directed solely at her mouth. "Don't you believe in love, Maddie?"

She wished he wouldn't stare at her mouth. It was unnerving and half tempting. She had firmly placed Morgan in a nice little box marked "Father's Business Associate" and that was where he was going to stay. "I love my father very much."

"I wasn't referring to family love, Maddie. Don't you believe in the kind of love that happens between a man and a woman?"

She glanced out the window next to their table, at the rolling green of the golf course. Did she believe in love? Definitely. She had seen its destructive power and wanted no part of it. She watched as a pair of golfers set up for their shots on the eighth hole. "Yes, Morgan, I believe in love."

"You don't sound too happy about it."

"Love nearly destroyed my father, when my mother died." The second golfer took his stance and teed off. She could feel Morgan's intense gaze on her face, as if he were trying to read every emotion. He would see nothing she didn't want him to see. She was an actress both by profession and by choice. "I really have no desire to know that particular feeling."

"Some men would take that as a challenge, Maddie."

Her gaze jerked away from the window and collided with his. "Some men were born fools."

Morgan laughed. It was a rough sound that attracted some attention from the diners around them and made her want to smile.

"I can't argue that one with you." He finished his coffee and smiled. "You've been surprising me, Maddie."

"In what way?" She didn't want to be surprising Morgan or any other man.

"You've grown into a very intelligent, beautiful, and desirable woman."

Oh, damn, Morgan was falling out of his box faster than she could shove him back in. Morgan found her desirable and beautiful! Saints preserve her, she was about to melt into a gooey puddle of adolescent hormones. "Really, Morgan." She gave a dismissive wave of her hand as if his compliment meant nothing to her. "This is from a man who told my father I couldn't get a date because of the color of my hair?"

"I haven't noticed any temper to accompany that wonderful fiery shade of red."

"Maybe you haven't been around long enough." He thought her hair was wonderful. He was definitely out of his little pigeonhole box and running rampant over her intentions of distancing herself.

"And maybe you don't possess a temper." He reached out and brushed her fingers with his hand. "Have dinner with me tonight?"

She snatched her hand away so fast, she almost knocked over her water glass. She had nearly fallen for his smooth words and admiring looks, the snake. "My father put you up to this, didn't he?" She should have seen it sooner. Her father conveniently leaving her and Morgan alone, the nice restaurant, and the not-so-subtle hints all week long.

"What does your father have to do with me asking you to dinner?" Morgan looked confused, but she wasn't about to fall for that routine.

"He wants me married and producing little heirs." She shook her head and glanced over at her father, who had stood up and was saying good-bye to Brenda and her son. "You are his first choice in prospective sons-in-law, Morgan. You should be flattered."

"I asked you to dinner, Maddie, not to an exchange of vows for a lifetime." Morgan signaled a waiter for their check. "Are you always so distrusting, or is it just me?"

"During the past week I've had every one of your sterling virtues listed and categorized for me." She managed a weak smile for the waiter, who presented Morgan with the bill.

Morgan glanced at the amount and tossed a couple of large bills on top. As the waiter walked away, he said, "I guess I was mistaken."

"About what?"

"Your intelligence level. If you don't want to have dinner with me, fine, just say so. But don't blame it on your father, Maddie."

"Fine."

"Fine what?" Morgan stood up and helped her from her chair.

She nodded politely at Morgan for the benefit of her approaching father and the half-dozen people whose entire lunch seemed to have been dedicated to watching her. She leaned in closer to Morgan and whispered, "Fine, I don't want to go out with you."

She turned away from him and smiled at her father before glancing at her watch. "Good, you're back. We'll have just enough time to drop Morgan at his office before heading in for your therapy session." Without looking back at Morgan, she headed out of the restaurant as if she hadn't a care in the world.

Any moment she expected the crowd to stand

up and cheer her magnificent performance. Morgan had her stomach twisted in so many knots she'd nearly forgotten her lines. She had almost told him yes, she would have dinner with him. What a disaster that would have been.

FOUR

Morgan followed a boy's waving arm and turned onto the grass field and parked his car. A green minivan immediately parked beside him. Half a dozen teenagers, all dressed in Elizabethan costumes, piled from the van and raced toward the gate of the Pennsylvania Renaissance Faire. Whatever had possessed him to travel to Mount Hope to visit one of the county's leading tourist attractions? He could answer that with one word: Maddie.

Madeline Andrews was causing him to do the most unpredictable things. When he had stopped in at Glen's that morning to see how the older man was doing—and, if he was honest, to spend some time with Maddie—he had been pleased and not surprised to find Brenda keeping Glen company. Maddie wasn't there, however. She had gotten a job, Glen told him, at the annual

Renaissance Faire. And, Glen went on, she needed a ride home that evening. Her van was in the shop and she had managed to secure a ride to the Faire with a fellow actor who lived in Lancaster and was playing the part of Sir Francis Drake. Maddie could ride back home with the actor, but Morgan decided he would pick her up. There was something about Maddie carpooling with Sir Francis Drake that rubbed him the wrong way.

Although Maddie worked until six, he decided to spend the afternoon at the Faire and see exactly what Maddie was up to. Glen had explained a little about the Faire, enough to pique his interest. He knew all the entertainment was staged, but he was still curious enough to want to see an actual joust. He had also heard some wonderful compliments regarding the various vintages of Mount Hope wines. The Faire was located on the same property as the Mount Hope Estate and Winery. Not only was there the Faire to see, but also a tour of the Mount Hope Mansion and formal gardens, which had been built in the eighteen hundreds. The vineyards had been planted only seventeen years ago, but the reputation their wine was receiving was remarkable.

As for Maddie, he wasn't sure what to make of her and her chosen career. He knew Maddie's mother had been an off-Broadway actress who had met Glen while visiting relatives in the area. The upper crust of Lancaster County had been scandalized when Glen broke off his long-

Here's Lookin' at You

standing relationship with one of the "darlings" of the social set and married Carolyn within a month of their first meeting. Even more than thirty years later, some of the most prominent matrons still snubbed Glen for having married an *actress*.

Personally, he thought the whole thing was ridiculous. Glen and Carolyn had obviously been very much in love and deserved whatever happiness they had found. It was the same social snobs who had been fanning the flames over Maddie's career choice ever since her return. He could think of a dozen occupations Maddie could have chosen that really would have had the tongues wagging. Acting wasn't one of them.

As he got out of his car, he noted the bright yellow and green banners blowing in the breeze that marked the path to the entrance gate. A couple, holding hands and laughing, hurried up the path. At least they were dressed in regular clothes and not costumes.

He only had Glen's and Brenda's brief explanations to prepare him. Actors and actresses dressed and acted the part of the citizens of a merry shire during Elizabeth's reign in England. There would be the queen, and of course her court, Sir Walter Raleigh, and a host of other nobles. Then there would be the Spanish Court, as King Philip II has come to England to try to win the hand of the Virgin Queen. All the other actors portrayed ordinary working people and rabble who roamed the Faire and entertained the patrons.

Hanging out with "rabble" wasn't his usual form of entertainment, but it did spark an interest. Anything Maddie did was sparking an interest. In the week since he last saw her and her father at lunch, he had done little but think about her. She sure wasn't his sister's pesky little friend any longer and he really wouldn't mind at all if she cornered him out by the pool again. In fact, he would guarantee a completely different outcome to that encounter.

He followed a boisterous family to the ticket booth, purchased his ticket, and frowned at the stone archway everyone had to pass through to enter the Faire. The stone archway didn't bother him. It was the dirty, rag-covered beggar sitting directly in front of the entrance spouting tales of sin, wickedness, and merriment beyond the walls that gave him pause. So this was the "rabble." He had to grin at the young man, who had most of his teeth blackened out. It was one hell of a way to make a living.

As he passed under the archway, he glanced around curiously at the crowded dirt streets. People, half of them dressed in costumes and half of them not, strolled from shop to shop. He couldn't tell the actors from the patrons who wore costumes to save two dollars off the entry fee. Food seemed to be the specialty of the row of shops directly in front of him. The air was full of voices, laughter, and the smell of grilling sausage and other delicious scents.

His stomach's rumblings reminded him that it was past his usual lunchtime, but instead of heading in the direction of the tantalizing aromas, he turned toward the information booth directly to his left. The first thing he had to do was find Maddie and let her know he would be taking her home that evening, not Sir Francis Drake. Finding her in this crowd might take some doing, especially since Glen hadn't told him who she portrayed. Without the first clue as to where to look for her, it might just take him the rest of the afternoon to locate her.

He approached the Tudor style building marked "Informistress" and listened with amazement as the costumed young man gave a weary-looking mother and her two small children a detailed list of shows appropriate for the "little nippers." The amazing part was the clerk never once spoke in modern-day English, yet Morgan and the thankful mother understood everything he said.

"How may I serve you, gentle squire?" the young man asked Morgan.

"I'm looking for one of the actresses, Madeline Andrews." He could detect a questioning look behind the clerk's practiced smile. He had to wonder how often men inquired about certain actresses, and Maddie in particular. "I'm her ride home tonight and I wanted to make sure she knew I was here before I enjoy the Faire."

"You'll be needing the program then, *Elizabethan Times.*" The man picked up a colorful brochure with a knight riding a charging horse printed on the cover. " 'Tis a must for every Faire goer. It explains all the comings and goings of the den."

He paid for the program and asked, "What about Madeline?"

" 'Tis Yewanna, the sensuous vixen, you be seeking." The man quickly glanced at his watch discreetly hidden under the long sleeve of his tunic. Waving his arm, he pointed to the right and up the dirt street with all the food shops on it. "Hie you up Ha'penny Hill to the Boarshead Inn. The merriment upon the stage hath just begun."

Morgan frowned at the term "sensuous vixen." It sounded a bit too personal to him. He took it that Maddie was playing a person named Yewanna and whatever she did onstage was just beginning. "Thank you." He turned to the street, but stopped as the young man called out to him once more.

"Be ye warned, the Boarshead Inn is not for thy Puritan soul. The shire is a hotbed of sin and wickedness and they sayeth Satan's lust dwells at the Inn."

Morgan didn't like the wicked and meaningful grin the clerk threw him. Why was the guy warning him about sin and wickedness when all he was doing was trying to locate Maddie? The Pennsylvania Renaissance Faire was family entertainment; how much sin and wickedness could there possibly be? "Thanks for the warning." He once again turned in the direction of the Boarshead Inn and strode up the crowded street. If Maddie was performing onstage, he definitely wanted to be there, especially if sin and wickedness were involved.

He had to wonder who, or what, she would be. In his opinion, and knowing that she had been acting in a Shakespearean play in Connecticut when her father had taken ill, he would have guessed nothing short of the role of Queen Elizabeth herself would do for Maddie. But then again, he was being prejudiced, for he knew Maddie. Besides, the clerk had said Maddie was playing the part of someone named Yewanna. The queen's name was Elizabeth.

Morgan passed the tempting Ye Meat Inn, where the sizzling sausages made his stomach rumble once again. As soon as he had spoken to Maddie, he really was going to have to do some serious investigating along Ha'penny Hill. He flipped open the brochure to the center map.

The Boarshead Inn was directly in front of him, where a large, boisterous crowd had gathered. Whatever was going on onstage, it sure was attracting a lot of attention and laughter. It was so crowded he couldn't see the stage from the back of the seating area, so he worked his way around to the side, where the overflow of the audience was standing and merrily clapping along to a song he couldn't hear properly. It sounded something like, "Throw your leg over, 'tis better that way."

Morgan ended up at a spot slightly behind the protruding stage. It gave him a great view of the audience and the five actresses who were leading the crowd in a rollicking and risqué song that had to do about . . . Well, he hoped he was wrong about what it had to do about. By the audience's good-natured shock and laughter, he knew he wasn't wrong. The five women were singing about pleasures that could be bought, for the proper price.

His gaze fixed on the woman in the middle, who was commanding an unequal portion of the crowd's attention and laughter. Maddie! It had to be Maddie.

From his vantage point he could only see her back, but her height and her hair gave her away. No two women could be that tall and have that curly red hair that fell to just beyond her shoulders. Her bare, kissed-by-the-sun shoulders.

Maddie's arms were covered by off-white linen sleeves that started just below her shoulders and ended at mid-forearm. Her plain, dark green dress, or frock, covered her to her ankles and told him clearly that Yewanna wasn't one of the nobles. By the bawdy song she and the other women were singing and the suggestive swaying of her hips, he didn't need a vivid imagination to know what Yewanna's profession was. No wonder Glen had changed the subject that morning when he asked whom Maddie played. Who would want to admit his daughter played a sixteenth-century sex-for-hire vixen?

His fear was confirmed when a raven-haired beauty, dressed in a pirate costume that left the audience in no doubt of her voluptuous charms, called Maddie "Yewanna." Yewanna Synne to be exact.

The song came to a rousing end with a multitude of catcalls and whistles from the male population of the audience. The women sitting on the makeshift bleachers were either blushing or laughing. Not a child was in sight. He quickly opened his program to see exactly what type of performance Maddie was participating in. He wasn't surprised to see "Bawdy Ballads" printed in this time slot under the Boarshead Inn. Nor that this show was listed for "Mature Audiences Only."

He slowly closed the brochure and frowned at Maddie's back as she made a suggestive remark to the two petite blondes standing next to her. The women, dressed in what appeared to be their nightgowns, were presumably twins. Topps Aswaying and Bottoms Aswaying proceeded to give the crowd an earful on what exactly the males in the sixteenth century spent their time doing, and with whom. He had to smile as Topps and Bottoms made their way into the audience, trying to "raise" up some business. A person had to admire the girls' enthusiasm.

Yewanna was left onstage with the two other "working girls" who were complaining that Topps and Bottoms were getting first dibs on all the good-looking customers and that no one could beat their two-for-the-price-of-one sale. The trio immediately went into a hilarious number about the extravagant performance some men claimed, while Topps and Bottoms worked the crowd. Morgan couldn't help but chuckle along with the rest of the crowd at the medieval and bawdy version of the "fish that got away" tale. While Yewanna sang one verse, the serving wench, named Tastee Treet, kept moving her hands farther and farther apart. By the end of the song there wasn't a straight face in the audience.

He was beginning to see the humor in Maddie's choice of characters as the five women united on the stage to discuss Tastee's recent loss. It seemed the poor lass had just that morn buried husband number four and was already seeking a replacement. The whole show was done in harmless jest and not one of the tempting vixens showed an inch of scandalous skin. Not one vulgar word was spoken or sung, but put all together, what they said and did presented some very interesting possibilities.

Morgan stayed in the shade of a tree, hoping Maddie wouldn't spot him too soon. He wanted to see her perform without her being aware of him. He wanted the time to watch her unnoticed and appreciate her clear, sweet singing voice.

Her face was as beautiful as always. Sparkling green eyes, thick dark lashes, and a straight nose with those adorable freckles dusting it. Her mouth was generous, and the saucy know-it-all grin that she shared with various men in the audience went straight to his gut and angled its way lower.

The front of her gown wasn't low cut and in no way could it be classed as indecent, but it was tempting. He came to the conclusion it had to be the frayed yellow ribbon lacing its way up the front and tied into a loose bow just where the swell of her breasts began. There was only a hint of cleavage, nothing too seductive to entice the male patrons. So why did that damn bow tempt his fingers to give it a good yank?

By the looks on some of the other men's faces, they suffered from the same temptation. He glared at the thin yellow length of satin as Maddie laughingly patted an elderly bald man on the head and complained about cold sheets and empty purses. Damn that frayed ribbon!

He knew the instant she spotted him. She must have sensed his gaze, because she immediately turned and stared right at him. She missed her next couple of lines, but Topps—or was it Bottoms?—covered for her nicely. He wasn't sure if he should be flattered or worried that his presence had caused her to flub what had been a perfect performance. By the murderous look in her eyes, he didn't think he should go out and celebrate quite yet. He had a feeling he was going to pay for disrupting her concentration.

Maddie turned her back on him and picked up her next lines as if nothing had happened. Still singing, the five temptresses left the stage and worked their way through the audience with a smile on their lips and a swaying of their hips. Every male received a smile, or a look, or a finger trailed up a forearm, or a knee suggestively patted while they sang verse after hilarious verse.

Tastee was heading to the far portion of the crowd, where he was standing, when Yewanna cut her off. There was a purposeful glow in Maddie's green eyes and an even more extravagant sway to her hips as she walked straight toward him. He could feel the attention of the crowd swing their way, and he frowned. Maddie might be an actress and crave the attention and limelight, but he didn't. He took a step back as she steadily approached. He wasn't positive, but he thought she licked her lips with anticipation. His retreat was spoiled as the trunk of the tree slammed into his back. He remembered too late that Maddie hated surprises.

"He's mine! I laid eyes upon him first," Tastee whined good-naturedly to the crowd.

Yewanna stopped directly in front of him and turned to Tastee and the audience. "Nay, he be mine if his purse be full." She flipped her hair over her shoulder and pouted sexily at him. "My sheets be cold and my blood be hot! What say you, squire?"

He couldn't believe this was the same woman who just last week had told him she didn't even want to go out with him. Now she was proposing a lot more than dinner and a movie.

"By my troth, Yewanna, he's enough for two! Me good mother always said to be a-sharin'."

Yewanna pressed herself against him and toyed with his hair at the nape of his neck. He was going to throttle Maddie when she was done having her fun at his expense; just as soon as she stopped playing with his hair and crushing her breasts against his chest. He felt the heat of her body and smelled the scent of her perfume. Glancing down at that faded yellow bow, he wondered what exactly would happen if he did give in to temptation and yanked the end. Had bras even been invented in the sixteenth century? He didn't think so, but surely the women back then wore something under their dresses.

"Surely ye jest!" Yewanna cried. The tip of her finger outlined his ear as she grinned unabashedly at the audience and Tastee. "Ye mother 'twas ne'er good."

"Fie on thee for breathin' me sainted mother's name!" Tastee exclaimed as she implored the audience for some understanding.

Yewanna rubbed against him as if she were a cat and he were a hot, sunny day. If he had been sitting, she would have been curled up on his lap and purring. He wasn't complaining, but he did wish she could have picked a more private setting to throw herself at him. He could only control his desire for so long, and his body was already hardening.

"Sainted!" Yewanna threw back her head and laughed. " 'Twas not what the archbishop sputtered the night he be caught hurrying from her bed."

Thankfully Maddie moved back a step, putting a few inches of space between their bodies.

"At least she had been beauteous enough to tempt a man of the cloth." Tastee seemed quite pleased with the woman who had given her life.

Yewanna turned to the crowd and winked. "Rumor has it the archbishop hadn't a cloth on him." The crowd roared with laughter.

Tastee puffed out her well-endowed chest, patted her chestnut-colored hair, and grinned. " 'Tis said I look like her."

"Zounds! Ye mother swelled more oft than the sea, buried twelve husbands, and populated half the shire of Hogsdale before the angels carted her off to her reward!" Yewanna turned away from him and hugged her friend. "Men are such scoundrels!"

"Aye, they be that." Tastee waved her fingers at him over Yewanna's shoulders and the audience once again erupted in laughter. "All they think about is food, drink, battle, and a willing wench." This time she winked and raised her ankle so he and the crowd could get a better view of her nicely turned leg.

"Not a wit toward our gentle feelings." Yewanna released her friend and joined the other temptresses onstage. "Men! They be all the same betwixt the sheets."

Tastee stood torn between the stage and him. "Yewanna, dear cousin, an' ye don't want him, I beg thee for him."

Yewanna rolled her eyes while shaking her head, and hauled the tempting Tastee Treet onto the stage. "Nay, mine dear cousin. We've labors afore us and he would only get in the way."

Tastee appeared disappointed until she spotted a broad-shouldered young man sitting in the front row. She literally beamed at him. The blond-haired, blue-eyed giant beamed back. "What say you I take him?" Her gaze slid suggestively down the man's body and landed on his lap. "He appears to have a full purse."

Yewanna elbowed her in the side. " 'Tis not his purse you be espying."

The blond giant blushed scarlet but Morgan didn't have much sympathy. He was too thankful that Yewanna and Tastee had finally left him alone.

He had to wait ten minutes after everyone had left the Boarshead Inn for other amusements before Maddie approached him. "Why be you here, Squire Morgan?"

"Your father told me about your broken muffler and I offered to give you a ride home this evening." He glanced at the group of people heading into the Scriptorium and Abbey across the way. "I know you already had a ride home, but I thought I'd spend the afternoon enjoying the Faire. I've never been here before."

She frowned. "Where be mine father?"

"He and Brenda Benson looked like they wanted to make some plans for just the two of them, so I left."

Maddie glanced at Topps and Bottoms as they headed for Bosworth Field. "I must hurry. I thank ye for the ride."

"Where should I meet you and when?"

"Six o' the clock at the Kissing Bridge."

He liked the sound of that. He was meeting a seductive vixen named Yewanna Synne at the Kissing Bridge. "By the way." He glanced at that damn yellow ribbon and grinned. "My purse is full."

For the first time since his arrival, Maddie stepped out of character. "In your dreams, De Witt." She turned and hurried after Topps and Bottoms.

Morgan's grin faded as he watched her walk away. No one was around to hear him whisper, "My dreams weren't nearly good enough, Madeline Andrews. I want you for real."

FIVE

Maddie made her way through the nearly deserted Faire to the Kissing Bridge and Morgan. She was fifteen minutes late. Seventeen years earlier she would have sold her soul to the devil himself to have Morgan waiting for her at a kissing bridge. Now, she was filled with nothing but unease. There had to be a reason for Morgan being there. She just hadn't figured it out yet.

A fellow actor was supposed to be giving her a ride home. Most people would have left it at that, but not Morgan. He had gone to visit her father that morning, learned she was hitching a ride, and driven all the way up here to drive her home. It didn't make sense. As far as she knew, Morgan did nothing that didn't make sense, very good sense. So what was the reason behind this spur-of-the-moment offer?

She cut across Guildmen's Way and spotted

the wooden Kissing Bridge. Morgan wasn't on it. It took her a moment to locate him. He was sitting under a towering oak tree enjoying the early evening sunshine. She took her time studying him as she made her way past the Olde Worlde Inn and closer to the lone man beneath the tree. The brilliant green of the early fall grass and the sparkling blue of the sky created a magnificent background for Morgan's devastating looks.

Though he could never be called "classically handsome," every female who had reached the age of maturity was instantly aware of his presence. She had taken some good-natured ribbing from her fellow actresses after their afternoon performance. She would be eternally thankful that Morgan hadn't made an appearance during their next show, because she knew she would have been in for another half hour of unmerciful teasing, especially from Allie, who played Tastee Treet. Not one of those women had believed Morgan was only a business associate of her father's.

Morgan looked relaxed sitting on the grass, twirling a leaf between his long fingers and studying the Tudor architecture of the reconstructed Globe Theatre. He looked like the average Faire goer, not the main force behind just about every blacktop road within a two-hundred-mile radius. He was dressed in jeans, sneakers, and a lightweight blue sweater. It was only early fall, but there was a definite hint of cooler air blowing down from Canada. A pair of sunglasses was perched on top of his head and his sleeves were pushed up his forearms.

He looked approachable and relaxed and that caused her to be wary. Morgan had never seemed approachable to her before. So what had changed? A simple outing to the Faire wouldn't do that to a man.

She reached the tree, tossed down her flower-print tote bag that contained every worldly possession she might need during an eight-hour work shift, and sat. "Sorry I'm late." She had changed into her normal clothes of jeans, blouse, and sweater and was no longer required to speak the Queen's English. The Faire had closed at six o'clock.

Morgan turned toward her and smiled. "I just got here myself." He leaned back on his elbows, crossed his ankles, and seemed ready to sit there for the next hour or so. "I never realized there was so much to see and do at this place."

"Did you get to see one of the tournaments at Bosworth Field?" She knew he had at least caught the last show, "The Trial by Combat." She had seen him sitting on Sir Michael's side of the audience, cheering on the green and gold knight. She, Topps, and Bottoms had been mingling with the supporters of the evil and eventually victorious knight, Sir George the Knight Slayer.

"I saw both the 'Tournament of Armes' and 'The Trial by Combat.' I must say they weren't very devoted to fair play back in the sixteenth century."

She chuckled knowingly. Fair play didn't enter into the tournaments at all. "We tend to take a few liberties to make it more interesting."

"I'll say. Poor Sir Michael was jabbed, slashed, maced, hacked at, knocked off his horse, and almost decapitated before he was pronounced dead. The man lost eight quarts of blood and was springing so many bloody leaks he looked like a garden sprinkler." Morgan shook his head. "I guess it was pure luck that he wasn't drawn and quartered to appease the bloodthirsty little nippers in the audience who were relishing every wound."

"Television violence has definitely made the fight coordinator's job more difficult." She leaned back on her elbows and studied a white fluffy cloud. "What else did you see?" Conventional wisdom said you could learn a lot about a person by what he or she read. Maddie figured the same principle should apply to which performances a person went to see at a Renaissance fair.

"I sat through the sword-swallower's show and couldn't figure out how he did it or even if he did it. The swords and knives looked real enough to me." He grimaced at the memory. "I watched the human chess match and a show at the Mudpit that was not only disgustingly dirty but hilarious as well. Nobody has enough money to pay me for what those poor guys had to do."

"I've only been here a week and I already know to stay away from the Mudpit." She plucked a blade of grass and stuck it between her lips. "What else caught your interest?" So far she hadn't gotten any deep insights into the working of Morgan's brain. He liked the tournaments or he wouldn't have gone back for the second show. The sword-swallower sounded dangerous and the chess match was a game of intelligence. All fit in with everything she already knew about Morgan. The Mud Games, however, seemed totally frivolous and out of character for him.

"Let's see," he went on, "I ate a cardiologist's nightmare for lunch, tasted complimentary samples of the queen's award-winning vintages, purchased a case of Her Majesty's best wine, and was embarrassed into buying a pickle from Saucy Susie and her traveling pickle cart." He nodded to the paper bag on his left. "I bought my sister a handblown glass ball that looked like it would fit right in with all the fancy bottles and knickknacks she likes to scatter on every flat surface in her house. I also checked out the blacksmith and weapon shop and admired a wicked double-blade sword with gemstones imbedded in the hilt."

"You didn't buy it?" The previous weekend, her first time working at the Faire, she had been positively amazed at the number of swords people actually bought. Swords weren't cheap by any means and it was an inside joke among the actors that the middle class was secretly planning a revolt against Washington and using the Faire as their weapon supplier.

"Oh, I wanted to buy it," Morgan said, "but for the life of me I couldn't figure out what I would do with it once I got it home."

She had to chuckle at the mental picture of Morgan wielding a sword during a business meeting. "Don't worry. It's all the male testosterone floating through this sixteenth-century air that made you want to buy an instrument of death and destruction."

"Put like that, I guess it would seem kind of arrogant and domineering to have the thing mounted on the wall behind my desk at work."

Saints preserve her! Morgan had a sense of humor. She could see the merriment gleaming in his dark eyes as he smiled at her. "You still might want to hang it there to serve as a motivational tool when things aren't going your way."

"I can see it now: Sign the bloody contract or taste the bite of my blade!"

She chuckled as he thrust his arm outward, as if he were wielding a sword. Maybe he should apply to replace Sir Michael, the fallen knight. The evil Sir George wouldn't stand a chance against Morgan, fair play or not. "Better be careful, Morgan, or someone might begin to think you're actually human."

The laughter faded from his eyes. He lowered his arm and stared at her. "You don't think I'm human?"

"I didn't mean it like that, Morgan." If she didn't know better, she would swear she now saw a vulnerability deep within his eyes. "It's just that I never associated you with having a sense of humor." The Morgan from her youth had been an experienced, mature college student who had humiliated her. Humor had never entered into her girlhood fantasies.

"What have you associated me with?" he asked.

She couldn't very well tell him the truth. She was well past the age of girlhood fantasies and crushes on friends' older brothers. "Hard work, a keen business sense, a friend and associate of my father, and a man filled with determination."

"Determination?"

"You didn't get where you are today without being filled with determination, Morgan. Not many twenty-two-year-old boys fresh out of college would have handled losing his parents and inheriting both a struggling business and a sixteen-year-old sister."

"Sometimes life doesn't give you a choice, Maddie. You work with whatever hand you're dealt." He looked away as if something else had captured his attention. "So if a man's hardworking and a success, it means he has no sense of humor and isn't human?"

"No, it means he has a friend with an idiot for a daughter." She smiled as his head quickly turned back in her direction. By the look on his face she would have to say she had startled, if not shocked, Morgan. "Hi, I'm Madeline Andrews and sometimes I can be a real idiot."

"Want to tell me why you think you're an idiot?"

"Not really, but I will." There was a lot she didn't want to tell Morgan, but she owed him something because of that not being human crack. Now that she was home to stay she would undoubtedly be running into him often. She glanced up at the deep green leaves of the giant oak. "I don't like beating around bushes, Morgan, so if I'm a little blunt, sorry.

"Seventeen years ago I had a schoolgirl's crush on you which you managed to squash quite effectively. My opinion of you back then didn't include your being human or even nice. Distance and years have taught me quite a few things, one being that your . . . let's say, rejection of my affections, was warranted and, in hindsight, greatly appreciated." At fifteen she had confused lust with love. Morgan had been the first boy she had ever wanted to kiss.

"Maddie, about that afternoon . . ."

She cut him off before he could finish his sentence. "Forget it, Morgan. I have. That was a different lifetime and it's better left forgotten." She gave him a reassuring smile. "What I was trying to get at was that over the years I only saw you a dozen or so times and each occasion you were either buried in work or occupied with Georgia.

You hardly ever smiled and the other day in the restaurant was the first time I heard you laugh since you were twenty-one. I'd just plain forgotten what a wicked sense of humor you had when it came to teasing Georgia."

"For a long time, Georgia didn't want to be teased." Morgan picked up another leaf and started to shred it into tiny pieces. "She had a hard time accepting our parents' deaths."

"You didn't?" She had known Morgan well enough back then to know that his parents' deaths had devastated him.

"We all combat our grief in different ways. I had the business and the responsibility of caring for Georgia to keep me busy and push me forward." The leaf disappeared rapidly beneath his fingers. "Georgia needed me."

She had to wonder who had been there for Morgan. Surely he had needed someone or something. She knew what it was like to lose a parent. Losing her mother had not only devastated her, it had changed her life forever.

Morgan's life had changed too. He had gone from the charming, teasing older brother that she had fallen head over heels in lust with to this grown man whom she didn't have a clue about. The only thing she had in common with Morgan was her father.

"My father has constantly talked about you over the years. Our weekly telephone conversations weren't complete until he had filled me in on your latest achievement or your next daring business venture. Even during my quick visits home Dad usually drove me by your newest plant or made sure he pointed out your brand-new office complex. My father is very proud of you, Morgan."

"He's just as proud, if not more so, of you, Maddie. Over our occasional dinners or a round of golf at the country club, you're all he ever talks about, besides business. 'Maddie got the lead in this play or that play.' 'Maddie just moved to Chicago where she'll be starring in some play.' 'Maddie just moved to Pittsburgh.' 'Maddie's meeting me in New Orleans.' 'Maddie's gone to Toronto.' 'Maddie's moving to Connecticut.'"

"I'm not jealous, Morgan, if that's what you're thinking. Your relationship with my father is very special to him and I appreciate all that you have done and shared with him." Morgan had appeared embarrassed yet proud hearing about her father's praises. He also apparently knew every move she had made over the years. She had to wonder if he ever got tired of hearing her father sing her praises. She sometimes wished her father wouldn't bring Morgan mentally along when they met for a quick reunion in some distant city. Now her petty jealousy seemed trivial considering Morgan had been there when her father had needed someone.

She glanced around and noticed the Faire grounds had grown quiet and empty. Only a few stray actors and actresses were strolling about. "Are you ready to go?"

"Whenever you are." Morgan stood up and reached down a hand to her. "I have to stop at the Mansion on the way out. They're holding the case of wine I purchased."

She grabbed his hand and allowed him to help her to her feet. His hand didn't feel like that of a sit-behind-a-desk-and-pound-on-computer-keys businessman. His hand felt warm, rough, strong, and secure. He felt like he could hold her world together whenever it was in danger of crumbling. As he had the other night, when he pulled her into his arms and held her while she cried out thirty hours' worth of tension and fears.

She immediately dropped his hand. That night his embrace might have started out as a comforting gesture, but that wasn't how it had ended. By the time she stepped out of Morgan's arms, she had been anything but comforted. His arms had ceased to be a haven, and had become something more. Exciting, fascinating, and arousing were just three of the sensations that had slammed into her as her tears slowed. She had quickly gotten him out of the house and herself back under control, then she had written the whole experience off as a bad case of nerves. Now she knew she had only been fooling herself.

There was something about Morgan's touch that not only melted her body and stirred her senses, it connected with her soul.

It was a daunting experience. One she preferred to think about some more when Morgan wasn't standing right beside her and staring at her as if she had just lost her mind. She reached for her flowered tote. "Let's get going."

A half hour later they pulled into her father's drive. The ride home had been filled with inane conversations about the weather, her father's improved health, and the rapid growth in population and houses throughout the county. Brenda Benson's car was parked in front of her father's house. "You can drop me off here, Morgan. I'm all moved into the cottage and I can just walk back there."

"Aren't you going in?"

"No. Dad has company and I wouldn't want to disturb them." She was delighted that her father had finally started to have a relationship with a woman, after all these years. Twenty years was a long time for Glen to have grieved for his wife and her mother. No one had doubted her father's love and devotion to Carolyn. As Morgan had said earlier, everyone handled grief differently, and Glen Andrews had worn his grief on his sleeve for nearly twenty years.

However, it seemed her father's stroke had not only caused Brenda to realize what Glen meant to her, but had opened her father's eyes to Brenda. A day had not gone by since his stroke that they hadn't seen each other. Maddie couldn't have been happier for her father. He deserved every ounce of joy he could squeeze out of life.

Morgan pulled his car up behind Brenda's. "Do you park your van here? It seems a long way away from the cottage."

"No, there's a small dirt lane behind the garage that leads to the cottage." She reached for her bag and was surprised when she felt Morgan pull away from the front of her father's house and head for the lane. "You don't have to drop me off at my door. It's a real pain trying to turn around."

"I'm sure I can manage."

She had no doubt that he could. His expensive luxury car was sleek and compact compared to the big brute of a van that she traveled around in. "I was more worried about your scratching the paint with a branch of a tree or something." Morgan's car probably cost more than what she'd made in the past three years. Acting was something you did for the love of it, not for the money. She could barely stand to watch as he expertly maneuvered the car down the bump-riddled lane and parked next to the cottage.

"See, I didn't hit a thing." He turned off the ignition and stared at the stone cottage for a moment. "I see you've been busy."

She looked at her home. The cottage really had taken shape in the past weeks. She had spent all her free time either with her father or working on the cottage. It hadn't been too difficult to get her father to let her move into the small guesthouse. The choice had been either the guesthouse or a distant apartment.

Her father had had the water turned on, the electricity and furnace checked, and hired a carpenter. The carpenter had managed to unstick two of the windows, but one had to be completely replaced, along with the front door. The frame of the huge six-foot window in the living room had been rotted through, so Maddie had had a set of patio doors installed in its place to bring in more light.

She had painted the flaking white trim and the new front door sky blue. A heart-shaped vine wreath wired with brilliant silk flowers and ivy hung on the door and two clay pots overflowing with some of her father's pink geraniums stood on either side. The cottage looked cozy and inviting.

She glanced at Morgan. He didn't look like he was in a hurry to go anywhere. "Do you want to come in and see what I did with the inside?" She was quite proud of how it had turned out. "So far only my father and Brenda have seen it, and their opinions really don't count. Dad would tell me it was nice no matter what it looked like and Brenda's taste runs in the more traditional direction, even though she was very gracious when she took the tour the other day."

"What makes you think I'll give you an honest opinion?" Morgan opened the door and stepped out of the car.

Here's Lookin' at You

"You don't strike me as the false-praises type." She joined him on the slate path that led to the door. Unlocking the door, she gestured for him to enter first.

Morgan stepped into her house and glanced around in what appeared to be mild curiosity, but rapidly shifted to something more intense. She followed his gaze and nervously nibbled on her bottom lip. She wondered if he thought it was too much.

She had painted the dull beige living room a dazzling turquoise with blinding white trim. A white leather sofa, a television and VCR, and a floor lamp were the only furniture in the room except a couple of cardboard boxes filled with books and videotapes. The two brass birdcages sat in prominence on either side of the archway into the kitchen.

"Hamster brain," screamed José.

"Suck an egg . . . grawwwk . . . suck an egg!" added Manuel.

Morgan glanced over his shoulder at Maddie. "Do you still want my honest opinion?"

"I already know your opinion on José and Manuel." She couldn't prevent the laugh that bubbled up. José and Manuel had once again captured Morgan's attention. She guessed she should be thankful that was all they'd said. Their language sometimes wasn't for the meek or easily offended. "I believe it had to do with chestnut stuffing and cranberry sauce."

"It was gravy. Lots of gravy." Morgan glared at Manuel. "These old birds look mighty tough."

Manuel glared back at him and made a rude sound, like someone had just sat on a whoopee cushion. "Stick it in your ear."

Not to be outdone, José screamed, "Blow it out your—"

"José!" shouted Maddie. "Don't you dare say that word!" The months she had spent trying to retrain the birds to say nicer comments had obviously been a waste of time.

José bopped his head up and down. "Bad boy, bad boy."

"No, José was a good boy." She cautiously reached her finger into the cage and scratched him on the top of his head. They had bitten her one too many times for her to ever relax when she was in biting distance. "Pretty boy, José." She looked over at Manuel and grinned. "Manuel's a pretty boy too."

Manuel glared at the way she was favoring José and shouted, "Kiss a Wookiee!"

Morgan softly laughed and shook his head. "I guess he told you."

She raised her hand at Manuel and pointed her finger like an imaginary gun. "Bang!" It was Manuel's favorite game and he tended to ham it up every time she played it with him.

Manuel flapped his wings, squawked, and shouted, "He got me!" Then he made some ridiculous gurgling sound and tilted his head to the side as if he were dead.

Maddie clapped her hands and shouted, "Bravo, bravo!"

José, who had watched his fellow parrot's performance, pranced along the wooden perch that ran the length of the cage and cried, "Long live the queen! Long live the queen!"

Morgan rolled his eyes as José and Manuel both took a bow. "Are they members of the acting guild?"

"No, just Hecklers Anonymous." Maddie tossed her tote on the floor near the couch. "This room isn't completely furnished yet, but I'll get there." She headed to the bathroom and pushed open the door.

Morgan glanced into the small cubicle. His expression gave nothing away as he surveyed the room. What once had been a mundane, faded yellow bathroom had been converted into an aquarium. There were fish on the shower curtain, fish on the walls, fish on the rug, fish on the curtain. There were fish everywhere. Brilliant, tropical-colored fish were even embroidered onto the towels.

Morgan glanced at her. "I take it you like fish?"

"I think I might have gone a little overboard on the fish, but it brightens up the room and that was the effect I was going for."

"I think you succeeded. It's definitely bright."

"You don't like it?"

"I didn't say that, Maddie. I said it was bright." He backed out of the room and stood in the doorway of her bedroom.

He would never make a good actor, Maddie thought. His face was too expressionless. He would, however, make one hell of a poker player. She couldn't tell what he was thinking about the room. She had painted the walls yellow and polished the furniture until her arms gave out. The chenille bedspread was white with huge multicolored flowers on it and fringe all around its edge. A few throw rugs dotted the wooden floor and the driftwood lamp sat on the nightstand next to the bed. She had raided her father's attic and come away with a white bureau scarf, an old-fashioned slipper chair, a fringed floor lamp, and her mother's silver-plated brush and comb set. All in all, even though the room looked straight out of the fifties, she thought it had a peaceful quality about it.

"Did you have a fixation with the television series *Happy Days* or are you working with what you have?"

"A little of both." So far neither of his comments spoke of praise. "If you don't like this room, wait until you see the kitchen." The entire kitchen was also done in the style of the fifties, compliments of what was already in the cabinets and her father's attic.

"Stop putting words in my mouth, Maddie." Morgan walked away and headed for the kitchen.

It took her a stunned moment to follow. Morgan was one of the most exasperating men she had ever known. He knew she wanted his opinion, but instead of commenting throughout the house, he was going to wait until he had inspected every nook and cranny before giving his judgment. She had no idea why his opinion should matter to her, but it did. For some unknown and unexplainable reason, she wanted Morgan to like what she had done with the cottage. She shook her head as she walked through the living room. It had to be her artistic temperament, as her father liked to call it, that was seeking Morgan's approval.

She stood in the doorway and watched Morgan survey the red and white room. "Well?"

He turned and faced her. "I'm still trying to figure out why it suits you so well." He took a step toward her. "I expected something contemporary or even the country style that is so popular right now."

She didn't understand the gleam in Morgan's eyes. It was a look that clearly stated he wasn't interested in talking about her home. As he took another step closer she could detect a hint of his aftershave. It was a brisk, clean scent that made her think of the ocean, and it had been driving her crazy the entire trip home. Her gaze landed on his mouth. His seductively tempting mouth.

"I think I figured it out," he said as he stopped directly in front of her.

She watched his lips move, but didn't understand a word he was saying. She wanted what her dreams had teased and tempted her with. She wanted Morgan to kiss her. "What did you figure out?"

His hand cupped her cheek and she forgot to breathe. His gaze roamed her face as if he were memorizing every detail. "Underneath that modern appearance of a very independent and worldly woman, you possess an old-fashioned heart."

She blinked. "Old-fashioned?" No one had ever applied that description to her before. She didn't want to be old-fashioned. She wanted to be sophisticated and brave and seductive. She wanted to seduce Morgan into kissing her.

His thumb softly stroked her lower lip. "There's nothing wrong with an old-fashioned heart, Maddie." He lowered his head and brushed a kiss where his thumb had just caressed. "In fact, I'm becoming very fond of one in particular."

She didn't even have time to catch her breath as he pressed his mouth over hers and kissed her in a very un-old-fashioned way. Her last thought was, would he still feel the same way about old-fashioned women if she swooned at his feet?

SIX

Morgan knew he was in trouble the moment he kissed her. The taste of Madeline Andrews not only lived up to his dreams, it surpassed them. Heat slammed into him like a sunny July afternoon in New Orleans. It steamed into his pores and scorched his gut. Maddie was burning him up from the inside out. Her body pressing up against his was the fuel and her delectable mouth was the match.

He gathered her closer to deepen the kiss and rejoiced in her heat. His tongue swept deep within her mouth and explored her sweetness. A kitten-like purr vibrated in the back of her throat. Delicate hands wrapped around his neck and tugged him closer. He would have shouted for joy if his mouth weren't so busy devouring hers.

Her plump breasts flattened against his chest and her teeth nipped at his lower lip. Her tongue danced seductively with his, arousing him further. His hands roamed her back and outlined the tempting fullness of her hips. Slim and graceful curves filled his hands as he cupped her bottom and pulled her against his jeans and the hard throbbing ache they contained.

He wanted Maddie with an intensity that not only caused his body to tremble, but his soul to ache. Never before had he felt this terrible vortex of need. His gut was telling him that no matter how intimate he became with Maddie, he was never going to be satisfied. Maddie was a deep, deep well; if he fell into her, he would never reach the bottom.

Her hot fingers stroked his shoulders and back while her mouth explored his with delicious wickedness. He had meant the kiss to be an innocent expression of his intentions. What exactly his intentions had been he wasn't too clear on right now. They seemed to have been incinerated by the fire of her response.

He needed to slow things down or food wouldn't be the only thing cooking in her kitchen. Right about now he felt like a barbecued chicken. A well-done barbecued chicken.

He had to remember this was Glen's daughter before he pulled her down onto the floor. He released her mouth and trailed a string of kisses down her throat to the collar of her blouse. Her skin felt like hot silk and his recently regained control was in danger of faltering once again.

Here's Lookin' at You

This was Maddie in his arms. He had known her all her life. Their parents used to play bridge at his house on alternate Wednesday nights, and he had been stuck with two little pests invading his room, instead of just Georgia.

Maddie pulled him closer as he tried to pull away. He raised his hands and tenderly cupped either side of her head. His fingers wove through her silken curls as he studied her flushed face. Her breathing was shallow and rapid, her lips swollen and reddened by his kisses. He felt his heart slam against his rib cage as she opened her eyes and gazed up at him. Green fire burned behind her thick dark lashes.

Maddie wanted him as much as he wanted her. That knowledge should have made it so simple, but it didn't. A lot of issues stood between them and her bedroom door.

His thumbs slowly stroked her smooth cheeks, and the enticing scent of her perfume tugged at his resolve. Yewanna Synne would have been one very rich woman back in the sixteenth century. Rich and busy. He, however, wasn't looking for a couple of hours of quick enjoyment and release. With Maddie he sensed something special. Contrary to her daring portrayal of Yewanna and her independent ways, she did possess an old-fashioned heart. One that matched his perfectly.

"Maddie, I'm not very good at one-night stands." He almost smiled at the way her eyes widened. Either she didn't believe him, or she had just realized where they'd been heading. He brushed her moist lower lip with the pad of his thumb. "I would give quite a lot to know what you're thinking at this moment."

She blinked twice and hastily took a step back. "Save your money, Morgan. I'll tell you what I'm thinking." She put more than a few inches between their bodies. She appeared to be aiming for the entire length of the kitchen. "That shouldn't have happened."

"Why not?" He knew of a few reasons why they might want to think about any relationship they might have, but none would put that particular look on Maddie's face. She looked one-third aroused and two-thirds appalled.

"You're the son my father never had," she said.

"That doesn't make me your brother, Maddie. I already have one sister, I'm not looking for another." He'd known Glen would be a stumbling block in any relationship he might build with Maddie. "I don't think your father would object to us seeing each other."

In fact the complete opposite was true. A couple of weeks ago Glen had been tossing out hints, even commands, for grandchildren; quarry-business-minded grandchildren to be more precise. Maddie hadn't seemed too keen on delivering those much anticipated grandchildren. He had to sympathize with her. No one would appreciate being told when to start having babies. Glen had tried to be a little diplomatic about his wishes, but there really wasn't any polite way of saying, Start producing an heir or two.

"My father would not only have no objections, Morgan, he'd be calling the caterers and ordering up my wedding dress so fast, it would make the gossip mill at the country club seem positively slow." Maddie shook her head at the mere thought of it. "You'd be trussed up in a tux, standing before a preacher, and stumbling over the words 'I do' before you had your first thoughts on the matter, let alone second ones."

He had to chuckle at that absurd picture. "I don't think your father will be marrying you off to the first man you date, now that you're home."

"We're not talking about any man, Morgan. We are talking about you." She swept up a few fallen petals around the flower arrangement sitting on her kitchen table and threw them in the trash. "Your asphalt genes mixed with my quarry genes would be the perfect combination. My father wouldn't be able to help himself from dreaming of an heir."

Morgan couldn't prevent himself from gazing at her long, trim legs and the enticing curve of her hips. The words "Maddie" and "jeans" in the same sentence elicited only one reaction from him—instant lust. "I don't see anything that even resembles a quarry in your jeans."

Maddie fought a smile and won. The smile faded. "I'm sorry, Morgan. You're a nice man and all, but I'm just not in the market for a relationship right now."

He raised an eyebrow at that. Not too many people referred to him as nice. Years ago Georgia had christened him with the private nickname of Marshmallow Heart. The nickname was a closely guarded family secret, because if the business community ever got wind of it, his reputation would be ruined. Who in their right mind wouldn't try to take advantage of someone called Marshmallow Heart?

"Are you seeing someone else?" he asked as a new thought slammed into him with the force of a hurricane. "Is there someone up in Connecticut who owns a piece of your heart?"

"No, there is no one in Connecticut or any other state."

Okay, so there wasn't a lover waiting elsewhere for her return. "As I stated before, you're a beautiful, intelligent, and desirable woman, Maddie." He leaned against the chrome and Formica table and studied the frown creasing her forehead. "I'm having a hard time accepting the fact that you don't date at all. I know since your return you've been busy worrying about your father, settling in here, and starting a new job. Glen has recovered nicely, the cottage looks great, and I've seen you portray Yewanna with more zeal than I cared for you to display. So time is not a factor."

He tried to read her face, but it was such a mass of different emotions he couldn't tell which

Here's Lookin' at You

were real and which were a product of her acting abilities. "The only thing left is a broken heart."

"Whose broken heart?"

"Yours." He was an expert on broken hearts. He knew what they did to a person.

Maddie blinked like a big fiery-haired owl. "I'm sorry, Morgan, but I don't have a broken heart."

"So why the no-dating rule?"

"I didn't say I don't date. I said I wasn't in the market for a relationship. There's a difference."

"Good. Have dinner with me tomorrow night."

"No."

"Lunch?"

"No."

"A movie? Breakfast? A walk on the beach?"

"No, no, and there are no beaches in Lancaster County, Morgan."

"What about a romantic stroll along a reservoir?"

"I'm sorry, Morgan, but I can't go out with you."

"Can't or won't?"

"Both." She worried her lower lip, not meeting his gaze. "I don't think it would be a good idea."

He had done many things that some people might have said weren't a good idea in the beginning. Those same people eventually changed their minds. His instincts generally told him when to go for something, and when to back off. Every instinct he possessed was screaming at him this very instant. They were all telling him not to let Maddie call a halt to whatever might be, before it even began. Something was holding her back, but what?

"Can I ask you a question, Maddie? What are you afraid of?"

She folded her arms across her chest as she glared at him. "Who says I'm afraid of anything? Maybe I just don't want to go out with you. Surely your ego isn't that enormous that you can't stand a little rejection."

He had to give her credit. Her acting was superb. For a minute there, he actually considered she might not be as attracted to him as he was to her. The taste of her, still clinging to his mouth, told a different story. No one could have faked that response to his kiss. "My ego is just fine. So is my memory."

"I don't see—" A loud knocking on the kitchen door interrupted whatever she had been about to say. She threw him a look that dared him to say another word on the subject as she walked to the door and opened it. "Hello, Dad."

"I'm not intruding, am I?" Glen looked curiously at Morgan standing in the middle of his daughter's kitchen and grinned. "Good, you haven't left yet. I see you got her home safely." He stepped into the kitchen as Maddie shut the door behind him.

"What are you doing here, Dad? I thought you and Brenda had dinner plans."

"We did, except my plans and hers didn't mesh. I had reservations at the country club and she shows up at the house with two bags full of groceries and some low-fat, low-cholesterol, low-everything cookbook. She's afraid I'm not eating properly when we dine out."

"Brenda's obviously very concerned about your health, Dad." Maddie wrapped her arm around her father's shoulders and kissed his cheek. "I think it's cute the way she fusses over you."

"You wouldn't have thought it was cute the way she just kicked me out of my own kitchen." Glen tried to look upset, but his smile ruined it. "She said I had to walk over here and invite both you and Morgan to dinner."

Maddie immediately shook her head. "I don't . . ."

"She said to tell you she has already made enough for the four of us and that dinner will be ready in twenty minutes."

Morgan could tell Maddie was thinking desperately of an excuse. Any excuse. "Come on, Maddie," he said. "One nutritious, low-fat, low-everything meal won't kill you."

"Are you saying I'm *fat*?"

He playfully threw up his hands and winked at Glen. "Not me, Slim. That's an *f* word that would never pass my lips where you are concerned. I was just trying to point out that Brenda has gone through quite a bit of trouble preparing our meal. The least we can do is eat it." As far as he was concerned Maddie's body was perfect.

Maddie glared at him for a moment, then turned her attention to her father. "Fine, we'll be happy to join you and Brenda for dinner." She walked over to the refrigerator and opened the freezer door. "I have Sinful Strawberry ice cream or orange sherbet I could bring for dessert."

"Brenda already picked up dessert." Glen walked over to the door. "We better get a move on it. I want to show you those mums I told you about the other day. They're in full bloom and they are gorgeous. I've never seen red like this on a chrysanthemum. Those cuttings were worth every penny I paid for them."

Morgan followed the glowing Glen and smiled at Maddie. "Coming, Slim?"

"Careful, Morgan," she said as she followed him and her father out of the door. "I just might not take that as a compliment."

Morgan chuckled along with Glen as they headed for the twisting and turning garden path to the main house. Twilight was deepening, and with it the promise of spending an evening in Maddie's company. It wasn't exactly how he had envisioned an evening with Maddie would be, but he wasn't foolish enough to complain. So far their stumbling block—Glen—had been more of a help than a hindrance.

Morgan hadn't felt so alive in years! The more

time he spent in Maddie's company, the more facets of her personality he uncovered. Madeline Andrews was beginning to look more and more like a diamond.

Maddie looked at her father and Brenda together and knew it was hopeless. She couldn't stay mad at him. He hadn't looked this happy in a long, long time. Twenty years to be precise. Maddie knew Brenda Benson would never replace Carolyn, but Brenda was filling her father's life with happiness and possibly love. Maddie hoped it was love, because she had been worrying about her father for years. He deserved so much more happiness in life and she knew her mother would never begrudge his finding love for the second time.

Watching him and Brenda during dinner, she wouldn't be surprised if there was a wedding in the near future. Maybe that explained some of her father's uncharacteristic behavior that night. His matchmaking attempts directed at Morgan and herself were not only blatant, they were downright embarrassing. Maybe it was a case of his wanting everyone to be as happy as he and Brenda were. The maddening part was Morgan seemed to be enjoying and possibly encouraging his every attempt.

Morgan was the one person she could direct her frustrations at. She needed to stay mad at him, because the alternative was just too disturbing to think about. Morgan De Witt made her want things she couldn't have.

When he had kissed her, she'd felt as if she'd finally come home. There had been passion and desire, but that she could have handled. She wasn't a virgin, after all. She had had a couple of lovers over the years, but none had broken her heart. She'd never risked her heart. She had had a great fondness and yes, even a form of love with the men who'd shared an intimate part of her life, but never the all-consuming love like her father had shared with her mother. She would never risk that. Devastation was a breath away from that sort of love. Morgan's heated kisses had shown her she'd be risking far more than just her body if she decided to pursue their mutual attraction. Her heart had actually answered his call, and that had shaken her to the core.

"Are you sure you can't stay longer, Maddie?" her father asked as she pushed back her chair. "We've barely finished dessert."

"Positive, Dad. I've got some stuff that needs to be done and I'm sure Morgan has things to do." She gave Morgan a look that dared him to disagree.

She walked over to Brenda and hugged the older woman. Brenda looked a good ten years younger than her age and no one would guess she was already a grandmother three times over. Tonight she was dressed in sage-colored slacks and a

Here's Lookin' at You

matching silk blouse. Her short dark hair was perfect, as usual, and her lively blue eyes sparkled with joy. Maddie prayed she would carry her age as well as Brenda. Next to the sophisticated woman, she felt positively drab in her jeans and sweater. "Thanks again, Brenda. The meal was not only delicious, it was enlightening." She sent her father a significant look.

Brenda hugged her back. "No thanks needed, Madeline. You're Glen's daughter."

"That doesn't mean you have to feed me, Brenda. You're already doing so much by hounding Dad about his diet and exercises." Maddie winked at her father. "He listens to you a whole lot better than he was listening to me."

"That's because," Glen said, "Brenda asks nicely, while you demand."

"Brenda hasn't realized yet just how thick that head of yours can be at times." Maddie kissed her father's cheek, pleased to note how much her father had improved over the weeks. He no longer needed a cane to walk and his face and speech showed no signs of the recent stroke. The only hint of weakness she had picked up on that night was a slight frailty in his left hand. Nothing that more therapy sessions wouldn't cure. "Good night, Dad." She smiled once again at the woman standing next to her father. "Brenda."

"Good night, Maddie." Glen extended his right hand to Morgan. "It was a real pleasure having you in for dinner, Morgan. We have to do it more often."

Morgan shook Glen's hand. "I will have to say, it was my pleasure, Glen. It's not every night that I get a chance to dine with two beautiful women."

Maddie opened the patio door leading to the terrace. "Morgan, are you coming or not?" She wanted to give her father and Brenda some privacy. She also wanted Morgan on his way home. The man was driving her crazy. The sooner he was several miles away, the safer she would be.

"Right behind you, Slim."

As she stepped out onto the terrace, her father flipped the switch for the outside lights, transforming the garden into a magical fairyland. Every path was discreetly lit and a few choice trees and shrubs were strung with miniature white lights. The gazebo and rose arbor were outlined in the same white lights. Her father's gardens were an enchanted place at night. One might expect to see spirited elves or pixies scurrying along the paths. It was also a very seductive place, filled with shadowy, intimate alcoves and tucked-away benches.

The patio door closed behind them and she started down the terrace steps. She knew the shortest way to the cottage. It was the path that skirted all the main attractions of the gardens. It didn't lead through the fragrant rose arbor or the secluded gazebo with its inviting thick-cushioned wicker furniture. The path she wanted to take avoided the white marble fountain depicting Rodin's "The Kiss." The last thing she wanted to see was two naked people entwined and kissing. When she was a little girl, she used to giggle at the statue encircled by gushing streams of water. The story was, her mother had once commented to her father about how she thought "The Kiss" was the most romantic sculpture ever carved. Within a month a replica of Rodin's masterpiece graced a secluded corner of her father's gardens. She turned toward the path to the left and was immediately halted by Morgan's touch.

"Let's go that way." He nodded to the right. "I haven't seen Glen's gardens at night for a long time. They appear so different with the lights."

She felt the warmth of Morgan's fingers as they entwined with hers. She tried to pull her hand away, but his was stronger. She could either make a scene over the gesture or just go along with it until they reached her cottage. She wasn't in the mood for an argument, so she left her hand in his and started down the path that would take them through the rose arbor. It was the safest route.

"Are you upset about your father's matchmaking?"

The lights from the house had faded behind a high wall of shrubs. The air had a distinct chill to it, but it didn't detract from the natural beauty of the grounds. Morgan's lingering pace left her no alternative than to go slowly and enjoy her father's gift of nature.

"Not as long as you don't take him seriously," she answered Morgan. She refused to meet his questioning gaze and instead concentrated on the path and the flowers that bordered it. "It was quite embarrassing, but I know deep down inside, my father means well. I think he's found something very special with Brenda and he wants everyone to know the same happiness." She could just see the rose arbor around the next bend in the path.

"They seem very happy together. Think anything will come of it?"

"You mean marriage?"

"I guess. I can't picture your father and Brenda 'living in sin.' "

"*Living in sin?* I didn't realize anyone still called it that."

"The world doesn't, but the self-appointed aristocracy around here has its own set of rules. Glen would never expose Brenda to that kind of scandal." Morgan stopped walking as they entered the arbor.

The miniature lights were just bright enough for Maddie to see the outline of his face, but not enough to read his expression. "My father would never subject Brenda or any other woman to the vicious tongues of some of those she-snakes who think they rule the world."

"I know about the scandal that rocked the

county when your father married your mother. I never could figure out what upset the she-snakes, as you so politely put it, more—the fact that Glen ended a long-standing relationship with one of the local debutantes, or the fact that your mother was an actress."

"Probably a little of both. Actresses are the kiss of death in their narrow Victorian minds. We're one step above prostitution."

Morgan chuckled. "I'm sure if Michelle Pfeiffer or Jane Seymour walked into the country club, the mobbing they would receive would be positively scandalous."

"True, but my mother wasn't a national celebrity. She was just a hardworking off-Broadway actress."

Morgan lifted his free hand and caressed her cheek with his fingertips. "Like you?"

"There's a big difference between my mother and me, Morgan. I'm not about to scandalize the county by marrying one of its most eligible bachelors." She turned her face away from his gentle touch and took a step in the direction of her cottage. Being in the dark with Morgan was a dangerous temptation. "I already horrified the poor bewildered dears enough by following in my mother's footsteps."

Morgan joined her as she continued along the path. "Is that why you've avoided relationships, because of a bunch of old busybodies with too much time on their hands and not enough gray matter?"

"If I were afraid of creating a scandal, I sure as hell wouldn't have chosen to follow in my mother's footsteps."

That much was true. Getting involved with Morgan, however, the crown prince of eligible bachelors, would only be asking for trouble. She could just imagine the nasty gossip that would engender, gossip that might hurt her father. It was all a moot point, though. She wasn't about to get involved with Morgan, or any other man for that matter. Marriage and motherhood weren't on her list of things to do in life.

Her cottage came into view and she quickly walked around it to the front driveway, where Morgan had parked his car. It was an obvious hint for him to go. She didn't dare look at him until they were standing by the driver's door of his car. "I want to thank you again for the ride home."

"You're welcome. Today turned out to be one of the most enjoyable days I've had in a long time." He leaned against the car and glanced at her cottage. "I take it I'm not going to be invited in for a nightcap?"

"There's not a drop of booze in the house and it's getting late." She very rarely touched the stuff. She had seen what it had done to her father after her mother's death.

Morgan nodded as if agreeing with her, but his next words belied that impression. "What are you afraid of, Maddie?" He captured her other hand and tugged her closer. "You either don't want a repeat of the kiss we shared earlier, which I don't think is the case because you enjoyed it as much as I did. Or, you're afraid you won't be able to resist if we do share another kiss." He pulled her up against his body and whispered, "Which one is it, Maddie?"

"Awfully sure of yourself, aren't you?" She glared at him and refused to think about the heat of his body warming hers to a soft, supple mass of want.

Morgan slowly shook his head. "You're mistaken there, Slim. With you I don't know which end is up. All I know is that you're the stuff dreams are made of." He cupped her chin and outlined her lower lip with his thumb. "I won't force the issue tonight, but I won't be pushed away that easily. I think there's something between us, Slim. What, I'm not sure, but I'm willing to take a chance and find out. Are you?"

"I don't . . ."

He lowered his head and stopped her words with a kiss that not only curled her toes, but knocked down a few more stubborn blocks that surrounded her heart. She couldn't resist the seductive dance of his tongue. Morgan De Witt's kiss guaranteed more than satisfaction, it promised paradise.

When she was so breathless and hot she thought she wouldn't be able to stand on her own two feet another moment, he released her mouth and broke the spell. She could see his dark eyes brimming with emotions that probably matched her own. They were going to be lovers. Sooner or later, it was going to happen. It was inevitable. Her heart was pounding a thousand beats per minute and her breathing was uneven, but she met Morgan's knowing look with a coolness she was far from feeling.

He gave her a small smile before brushing her lips one last time and gently pushing her away. Opening his car door, he nodded a good-bye. "Here's lookin' at you."

She felt a strange sense of being let down that he was just leaving like this. She doubted if she had an ounce of resistance left in her body or mind. "You forgot the 'kid' part."

He grinned as his hungry gaze traveled the length of her body. "I don't see a kid anywhere around." With those parting words he got in his car, backed out of her driveway, and disappeared down the dirt lane.

She should be furious at his audacity, but she wasn't. In an odd way she was flattered that he hadn't just given up on her when she told him she wasn't interested in a relationship with him.

The prospect of Morgan pursuing her should have made her seize up in pure panic. So why didn't it?

SEVEN

Maddie knelt next to the clay pot filled with wilted geraniums and sighed. She had done it again. Killed another innocent plant. She glanced at the matching pot on the other side of her front door and frowned harder. That plant had gone beyond wilting. It was now kindling. She wondered what she had done wrong this time. She had followed every one of her father's instructions to the letter and still the geraniums had died. It was hopeless. She was hopeless. Her thumb wasn't just brown, it was mortician black.

At the sound of a car coming up her lane, she glanced over her shoulder. She wasn't expecting anyone. Her father and Brenda were out and she had just gotten home from work. It was Saturday night and the only things she was looking forward to were a quick shower, a pair of baggy sweats, an old black-and-white movie in the VCR, and a bowl full of popcorn dripping with butter.

She recognized the car and sighed. Yewanna Synne had enticed, teased, and out-and-out vamped every male patron at the Faire that day. The last thing she needed was another male, but that was what she was getting. She watched as Morgan parked behind her van and got out of his car. It had been nearly a week since she had seen or heard from him. She still didn't know what to make of what had happened between them last Sunday night. She was beginning to think she had dreamed the whole thing.

Seeing Morgan now, she knew she hadn't imagined his potent kisses. Her body remembered the feel of his arms and the taste of his desire. No man had ever kissed her the way Morgan had. Her mind had been playing the 'What If' game all week. What if Morgan called? What if Morgan stopped by? What if Morgan kissed her again? The game had been mental torture, and it now looked like the game was about to become reality.

"Hello, Slim. You just get home from work?" Morgan asked as he walked over to her. His attention seemed to be fixed on the two pots of dead geraniums guarding her front door.

"About two minutes ago."

"What happened to the flowers? They looked fine the other day."

"I watered them." No use lying about it.

Morgan chuckled. "What did you water them with, ammonia?"

"Cute, De Witt." She wasn't in the mood to be insulted, especially by Morgan. The man had cost her too many hours of precious sleep this past week. "Did you come by just to laugh at my gardening skills, or was there another reason for your unannounced visit?" Morgan had absolutely no right to look so damned tempting. He was dressed in navy slacks, a cream-colored shirt, and a navy and cream patterned sweater. He looked fashionably casual for a fall evening.

She, on the other hand, had splattered mud up the side of her jeans and had forgotten to pack her brush in her bag that morning. The steady breeze all day long had made her hair look like something a family of mice had claimed.

"I came over to see if you wanted to go out to dinner," he answered. "I know you worked all day, so I thought something casual and relaxing." He jammed his hands into the front pockets of his pants. "There's a nice little Italian restaurant in New Holland."

Maddie frowned as she studied him. He wouldn't make eye contact with her and he was jiggling his keys in his pants pocket. Morgan was nervous about asking her out to dinner! The man had women standing in line just to be noticed by him, and here he stood on her doorstep acting endearingly sweet. She didn't have the heart to turn him down again, yet she really didn't feel like going out anywhere. "You up to throwing a couple of steaks on the grill?"

"Here?" The jiggling of the keys stopped.

The way the word "here" had stumbled out of his mouth, one would think she had just invited him to dance naked on her kitchen table. "If you have a problem with eating here, you don't have to stay." She picked up her tote bag, which she had set down while she examined the geraniums, and opened the front door.

He followed her into the house and closed the door. "Here's just fine."

"Good." She walked into the kitchen and pulled two steaks from the freezer. "Toss these into the microwave and by the time they're defrosted I should be done my shower." She left the room without waiting for his reaction. She didn't want to know if he was intimidated by a few microwave buttons. She had more important things to worry about. Like why Morgan had shown up at her doorstep to invite her to dinner, why she had countered the offer with one of her own, and why in the hell her heart seemed to be soaring.

Ten minutes and one quick hot shower later, she joined him back in the kitchen. She had nixed her favorite sweats for a clean pair of jeans and a baggy sweatshirt advertising the Broadway production of *Phantom of the Opera*. Morgan was leaning against the counter reading yesterday's newspaper, the two thawed steaks beside him. She gave the page that had caught his eye a glance.

The stock market. Figures. What was she thinking, that Morgan would be engrossed in the comics and chuckling over the Peanuts gang's latest adventure? "Lose any money?"

"Not yesterday." He refolded the paper and placed it exactly where it had been.

She took the steaks from the packaging and placed them on a plate. "Sorry, Morgan, but I have a hard time imagining you losing money on any day."

"Why not? Anyone who plays the market loses money occasionally. The secret is to make more than you lose."

"Hell of a secret. Care to share?" She started to pull the makings of a salad from the refrigerator.

"I might make more than I lose, but it has more to do with studying the market and pure luck than any secret." He snatched a tomato and tossed it into the air. "I really wasn't expecting you to cook for me, Maddie. Especially after working all day. If you didn't want to go out to eat, I could have picked up something and brought it back here."

She had to smile at the image of Morgan talking into some clown's head and ordering the value meal. She handed him the plate holding the steaks. "I'm not doing the cooking, you are. The grill's right out back. The microwave can handle the potatoes and I guess I can manage to chop up a few veggies for a salad."

"Sounds like dinner to me." He took the plate and headed for the kitchen door. "By the way, while you were in the shower Manuel called me a name that would cost me six Hail Marys if I repeat it."

"Did you tell him he was a bad boy?"

"No. I did mention something about grilling up some parrot-ka-bobs and washing his mouth out with soap."

She had to laugh. She knew what had happened next. Any time she threatened to wash Manuel's mouth out with soap he started singing "Tiny Bubbles" while bobbing his head up and down. "Did you enjoy his Don Ho imitation?"

"You have some sick birds there, Maddie. Did you ever think about getting them therapy?"

"Hey, I'm the one that taught Manuel that song." At Morgan's look of bewilderment her smile grew. "You should hear the cute little song I taught José. And no, I'm not going to tell you. You will just have to wait and be surprised."

Morgan shook his head. "If he calls me Hamster Brain one more time, I'll guarantee he'll never get a chance to sing it again." He closed the door behind him.

She continued to chuckle as she got two potatoes ready for the microwave. Morgan had been joking. She could tell by the gleam of laughter that had been sparkling in his eyes. Morgan was actually beginning to like her birds.

Maybe tonight wasn't going to be a disaster

after all. The whole time in the shower she had convinced herself that inviting Morgan to dinner was the equivalent of asking Satan himself. Nothing but trouble would surely come from the invitation. Now she wasn't too sure. All of a sudden she wasn't quite so tired after all.

An hour and a half later Maddie was snuggled up on the couch with a bowl of butter-dripping popcorn and an old black-and-white Humphrey Bogart movie just starting on the VCR. The only difference between this and the plans she'd originally had for her evening was Morgan. He hadn't figured in her plans, but there he sat, sprawled out next to her with his sock-covered feet comfortably resting on an upside down cardboard box. Her own black-and-gray plaid socked feet were mere inches from his.

"I still can't believe you've never seen *The Maltese Falcon.*" She shook her head in mock sadness at his deprived life. "It's a classic, Morgan. The next thing you'll be telling me is that you've never seen *Casablanca* or *The African Queen.*"

"Now there you are wrong. I did see *Casablanca* a couple of years ago."

"But no *African Queen*. No Katharine Hepburn. No Lauren Bacall in *To Have and Have Not* or *Key Largo*. How could you have gone through thirty-eight years of life without gorging yourself on Bogey? The man's a legend."

"He was just a man, Maddie. Flesh and blood, like the rest of us."

"Heck, that's like saying Lincoln was just a president or *Gone With the Wind* was just a movie." She looked at the television screen, where Sam Spade was sitting in his desk chair with the silhouette of the words from the plate-glass window ARCHER AND SPADE DETECTIVE AGENCY shadowing across the desk. There was something riveting about a black-and-white film. It was so undiluted that everything stood out crisp and clear. Shadows and moods were cast in gray. The director and actors couldn't rely on flashy colors to capture the audience's attention. They relied on talent, which Bogey had in abundance. She cursed the day Ted Turner had snatched up all the old classics and started to colorize them.

She glanced back at Morgan, who was already totally engrossed in the movie, and smiled. Bogey had done it again. *The Maltese Falcon* had been filmed fifty-six years ago, Bogey had been dead for forty years, yet they both still held the power to captivate their audience. "You have his eyes," she said.

Morgan turned his head and blinked at her. "Whose eyes?"

"Bogey's. You have Humphrey Bogart's eyes and his voice." She'd known there were similarities between Morgan's eyes and deep voice and Bogey's, but seeing them both in the same room brought the point home. It was almost uncanny.

"You're the second person who's told me that." Morgan shook his head. "Personally, I don't see it. Besides, Bogart's eyes weren't brown, they were a deep blue. They only look brown because of the black-and-white film."

"I'm impressed." Obviously, she was the only one, because Morgan's attention went right back to the movie. The man was impossible. She had just given him one of life's greatest compliments, comparing him to Humphrey Bogart, and he shrugged it off as if it were nothing. And who in the hell else had told him he had Bogey's eyes? It had to be a woman. Men didn't go around discussing eyes with other men, unless one of them happened to be sporting a shiner.

An hour and twenty minutes and a bowl of popcorn later, the movie was done and rewinding in the machine. Halfway through the movie she had gotten up to use the bathroom and to cover José and Manuel because they had started jabbering and it was their bedtime. Morgan had never once diverted his attention from the movie.

"So what did you think?" She was dying to know. It wasn't very often that she got a fresh perspective on Bogey. Most of her friends had cut their acting teeth on the old classics.

"It was one of the best movies I've seen in a long time," he said. "The story wasn't pushed along by graphic violence or blatant nudity and sex. Every other word didn't start with an *f* and it still was a great movie. Makes you wonder where Hollywood went wrong."

She grinned. She couldn't help it. The other day Morgan had told her she had an old-fashioned heart, and he had been right. Now she knew how he had spotted it. He had one himself. No wonder she felt so comfortable around him. "Can I ask you a question?"

"Sure." He lowered his feet off the box and stretched his arms above his head.

"Who told you you had Bogey's eyes?" The question had been eating at her during the entire film. Somehow, she didn't think it was his sister.

Morgan froze in mid-stretch. He seemed startled by her question, then resigned. His arms slowly lowered as he gave a deep sigh. "The same woman who watched *Casablanca* with me."

"Oh, now I see the connection." The woman would have to have been blind and deaf not to pick up on the similarities. She placed the empty bowl on the box and used the remote to lower the sound on the television. Some obnoxious salesman was shouting prices of washers and microwaves.

"Her name was Helen," he went on, "and I asked her to become my wife."

The remote almost slipped out of her hand. Morgan had asked someone named Helen to marry him! She'd heard rumors a few years back about Morgan and some woman, but she never paid much attention to gossip. As far as she knew, Morgan had never married. "What happened?"

He shrugged. "She said no."

Maddie blinked. *She said no!* Morgan had asked some woman to marry him and she said no! "Did she give a reason?" Or had she just been hauled away by men wearing white coats?

Morgan looked uncomfortable. "She was in love with someone else. Her husband."

"She was already married!" Morgan had asked a married woman to marry him? Good Lord! No wonder rumors had been flying around.

"He was her ex-husband. She'd been divorced for a couple of years when I met her and asked her to become my wife."

"How long did you date her before proposing?" She could tell he didn't want to talk about it, but she wanted the answers to come from him, not from some gossip mill.

"We dated for six months. When I popped the big question she asked for a couple of days to think it over. I knew she'd be hesitant, because she had been badly hurt the first time around. It seems my proposal made her realize how much she still loved her ex, and how unfair it would be to me if she said yes."

"What happened to her?" She could think of a few things she would like to see happen to the woman who had broken his heart. Morgan never would have asked her to become his wife if he hadn't been in love.

"She remarried her ex-husband and is living happily ever after."

Sometimes life was so damn unfair. "Do you still love her?"

"No."

Plain and simple, no. No explanation, no pools of pain flooding his dark eyes. Morgan had spoken the truth. His heart was healed and no torches were being carried. She knew how difficult it was to mend an old-fashioned heart. They took longer to recover than the average heart, and sometimes they didn't heal at all.

He reached out and touched her cheek. "Did you think I could kiss you the way I do and still love another?"

She swallowed the lump that had formed in her throat. Morgan's gaze had turned hot and full of want. She hadn't given it much thought. She hadn't had the time. "I haven't thought about that."

He slowly brushed her mouth with his. "I was born the day you kissed me."

His teeth gently nipped at her lower lip before he deepened the kiss. She melted faster than the butter she had poured over their popcorn. Morgan's nearness had been driving her crazy all night long. He had pulled his sweater off after he had finished grilling their steaks. The warm cotton of his shirt felt soft and inviting beneath her hands. The hard muscular wall of his chest made her fingers tremble. The rapid thudding of his heart matched her own.

What could a few more kisses hurt?

She felt his tongue sweep across her lips, and opened for him. Desire hardened the tips of her breasts and pooled between her thighs. With each bold thrust of his tongue she wanted more. She wanted the burning ache to go away. She wanted life to go away. She wanted to lose herself in Morgan's embrace and forget about the past.

She wanted to forget about all the reasons they shouldn't be tangled up in each other's arms and ready to christen her new couch in a way that would have shocked the poor salesman who had sold it to her. Morgan was the flame and she was the moth. She knew she was going to get burned, yet he was so irresistible. She wrapped her arms around his neck and pulled him down.

She tried to move her hips over, to give him more room, and was momentarily stunned by the hardness of his arousal pressing into her thigh. Morgan wanted her as much as she wanted him. Physical desire she understood. Love she understood too. Love had the power to cripple a person. Love had the power to destroy. There was only one access to love, and it was through the heart. Morgan couldn't touch her heart if she didn't let him. She was safe from love.

He broke the kiss and stared down into her eyes. "Maddie, what's wrong?" His voice was harsh and uneven.

"Wrong?" She wove her fingers into his hair and tried to catch her breath. Her heart was ready to pound its way out of her chest. She had never felt so alive. "What could be wrong?"

"You left me."

"Left you?" Why wasn't he making sense? Why wasn't he kissing her?

"Your mind drifted while I was kissing you." He brushed back a curl from her forehead and studied her expression.

"How can you tell?" She'd never heard of anything so preposterous. Her mind hadn't drifted, she had only closed off her heart to keep it safe. A person didn't need a heart to kiss.

Morgan sat up and pulled her to a sitting position next to him. After a long moment of silence he sighed heavily and said, "It's getting late, Maddie. I really should be going."

Maddie felt her jaw drop, and had to force herself to snap it closed again. *It was getting late?* It wasn't quite eleven o'clock on a Saturday night. Who was Morgan trying to kid? "You want to leave now?"

"No." He smiled gently at her. "But I am." He stood up and reached for his sweater, which he had thrown over the arm of the couch. "Thank you for dinner and the movie. Both were great and the company was exquisite."

She watched in amazement as he pulled the sweater over his head and straightened the collar of his shirt. What in the hell had happened? One minute he was kissing her as if he would never get enough, and the next he was saying good-bye. She stood up and straightened her sweatshirt, then brushed her hair away from her face.

She felt like laughing at the absurdity of it all. Hell, she felt like crying. Why was he leaving? She knew where all those passionate kisses had been leading. What she didn't know was what she was going to do when they got to a certain point. Her mind told her she was treading on very dangerous ground with Morgan. He'd never struck her as a light and fancy-free kind of guy. One-night stands or brief affairs didn't seem to be his style. They weren't hers either, and that was the problem. Her mind had been shouting for her to back off and put some distance between herself and Morgan, while her body had been, and still was, crying for his touch. Morgan De Witt would be one devastating lover.

She followed Morgan to the front door in a state of utter confusion. She should be thankful he had called a halt when he did, because if he hadn't, there might never have been a halt called. So why didn't she feel thankful?

He stood by the door, staring at her as if he had a lot on his mind and wasn't quite sure how to say it. Finally he pulled her into his arms and brushed her mouth with his. "Have dinner with me tomorrow night?"

With his mouth so temptingly close, how could she refuse? "I work until six."

"I'll pick you up at seven-thirty. We'll go someplace casual, okay?"

"Sounds great to me."

He kissed her again, but this time it wasn't a light caress. This kiss bordered on being possessive, and she was once again drawn to his flame. Just as she was ready to surrender everything she had, he broke the kiss and whispered, "Soon, Slim. Real soon."

She was left standing in the open doorway as he expertly turned his car around and drove down the lane. Frustration pulsed through her body and the taste of him clung to her lips. Morgan De Witt had just made a promise, one she knew would be kept.

Fifteen minutes later Morgan entered his house and turned on the lights. He glanced around the living room and to the dark archways beyond. Home was a comfortable two-story, four-bedroom colonial that his parents had built back in the early sixties. He had done some remodeling over the years and Georgia's hand could be seen in the decorating. It was a beautiful house, exquisitely decorated with an eye toward comfort. So why didn't it feel like a home?

When Georgia had lived there it hadn't been so bad. Now that she had a family and a place of her own, the rooms seemed to echo with loneliness. No one walked those rooms now except him and Norma, the cleaning lady who came in once a week. It was damned lonely. Sometimes, at night,

Here's Lookin' at You

the ticking of the grandfather clock in the hall made him want to throw something.

A few years earlier he had thought Helen would be sharing this house and his life. He had even dreamed about converting the small bedroom next to the master bedroom into a nursery. Helen had shattered those particular dreams, but not his ability to love. He had found out that startling fact tonight. He was falling in love with Maddie. Hell, he probably already was in love, but he was just being too cautious with his heart to admit it.

He made his way to the dark family room at the back of the house. He didn't bother to turn on any lights as he stood in front of the French doors leading to the back patio and the pool. The moon gave just enough light to distinguish the black tarp covering the pool for the upcoming winter from the white concrete that surrounded it. He wasn't seeing the pool as it was, he was seeing it as it had been seventeen years earlier that sunny afternoon when Maddie had so sweetly and awkwardly tried to kiss him.

Who would have thought that skinny fifteen-year-old girl with flaming red hair would be the one to bring love back into his life? Surely not he. Back then, Madeline Andrews had been a royal pain in his butt.

He was startled to see his smiling reflection in the glass of the doors. For the past sixteen years smiles hadn't come easily for him. First there had been his parents' deaths to deal with. Then Georgia hadn't snapped out of her grieving as everyone had said she would. Then there was his father's asphalt business. On the surface it had looked like a godsend. He'd been fresh out of college, needing to make a decent income to support himself and his sister, and was handed an established business. He'd learned quickly the falseness of silvery surfaces.

De Witt Asphalt had been floundering and about to go under for the third time. His parents, he discovered, had taken a second mortgage out on the house to pay for his college education. Their life insurance had covered the funerals and the monthly payments on the mortgages, but it wasn't enough to help the business. Pulling De Witt Asphalt back into the black had taken fourteen-hour days, six and seven days a week. When he wasn't at work, he was with Georgia, trying to help her cope. Those had been the worst years of his life, yet they were the years that had shaped him into the man he was today.

He now knew his own mind and how to get what he wanted. And what he wanted was Maddie. Physically he could have had her that night. She had wanted him as much as he had wanted her. The conclusion of their mutual attraction was obvious; they were going to become lovers. But something had stopped him, and that something was Maddie herself.

They had been in the middle of the most fantastically erotic kiss he had ever shared with a woman, when he realized something was wrong. Maddie was holding a part of herself back. It was as if she had mentally pulled from his reach the most vital part of herself. He had wanted that missing part. He wanted all of her. That was why he had ended the kiss and left in such a hurry. He didn't trust himself not to compromise his own principles and take only the part of her she had offered.

Maddie must have been hurt, and hurt deeply, by someone. He couldn't remember Glen ever mentioning anyone serious in Maddie's life. But there had to be a boyfriend, a lover, or even an ex-fiancé in her past who had broken her heart and made her leery of love. Maddie was a generous, intelligent, and loving woman. Her leaving her life in Connecticut to be with her father when he needed her was proof of that.

Someone had broken her heart and shattered her dreams. It was the only explanation he could think of. The other week in her father's study she had appeared positively certain she wouldn't be getting married. The subject of grandchildren had greatly upset her, even though she had tried to cover it. He wasn't sure if Glen had picked up on her distress. Maddie was one hell of an actress when she wanted to be, but her eyes had given her away that day. He had seen her pain.

Now he was beginning to piece together her reactions to her father's wish to pass Andrews

Quarries on to his grandchildren, but he still didn't understand them. Maddie had an old-fashioned heart, one that would naturally want a marriage and children in her future. One that would match his perfectly.

He turned away from his reflection in the glass door. He wasn't smiling any longer. Maddie needed a whole heart to love again and he had no idea how to mend her broken one.

EIGHT

Maddie waited patiently on the steps leading to the door of the country club's four-star restaurant while Morgan handed the parking attendant his keys. So much for a casual and relaxed meal after working all day. She gave Morgan a small apologetic smile as he joined her. It wasn't his fault, it was her father's.

That morning her father had been banging on her kitchen door before she even had the chance to finish her first cup of coffee. He had immediately issued her an invitation to join him for dinner that night at the club. She politely declined, saying she already had plans. When her father had questioned with whom, she'd told him Morgan. There was no sense hiding the truth from her father; he would eventually find out about her date with Morgan. And it was a date. Their first official date.

Her father had grinned widely at the news, but he hadn't seemed surprised. He told her he would contact Morgan and arrange for him to join them. Her father had something very important he needed to discuss with her, and since he considered Morgan practically part of the family, he was being invited along.

She allowed Morgan to escort her to the cloakroom, where she handed a perky-looking teenager her coat and received a ticket stub in return. She turned to Morgan and shrugged. "Sorry about this. I have no idea what my father wants to discuss, but he shouldn't have dragged you into it."

"As I said on the drive here, it's no problem, Maddie. We'll have dinner alone some other time. Your father sounded so excited on the phone this afternoon, I couldn't have refused him such a simple request." He reached for her hand and gave her fingers a light squeeze. "I still get dinner with you. What else could a man want?"

"Boy, and they thought Don Juan was smooth."

The maître d' greeted Morgan with respectful familiarity and immediately led them to their table.

Morgan bent his head and whispered provocatively, "Why is it that everywhere we go, you're always the most beautiful woman in the room?"

She shook her head as they crossed the dining room. "Better watch your step, Morgan. If my father hears you talking like that, he'll call out the chef and start discussing menus for our wedding reception." She wasn't so worried about how her father was going to respond to Morgan's sweet compliments; she was more worried about how she was reacting. So far she had broken every one of her good intentions where Morgan was concerned, and if she didn't watch her step, she was going to be in some seriously deep trouble. The man had an uncanny way of touching her heart. The same heart she'd sworn would never be touched.

"Brenda's with your father."

Maddie followed Morgan's gaze. Brenda and her father were sitting at a secluded table surrounded by towering palms and low lights. Her father's hand was covering one of Brenda's and they both looked ready to burst with happiness. The moment she reached their table, she knew what her father wanted to discuss. There was indeed a lot more than friendship going on between her father and Brenda, and she was thrilled for them both.

"Maddie, Morgan, it's about time you two got here," Glen said.

Morgan glanced at his watch and raised an eyebrow. "We're three minutes early, Glen."

"Seems like you're late," Glen grumbled good-naturedly.

Morgan held her chair as she sat. "It seems like you're in a hurry to spread some good news."

Morgan sat in the remaining seat, between Brenda and Maddie.

Maddie looked at Brenda and smiled. The poor woman was actually blushing. "I think I can guess the news, but go ahead and tell us anyway." She winked at Brenda. "Just in case I'm wrong."

Their waiter chose that moment to appear and ask if she or Morgan cared for a drink before dinner. She noticed her father and Brenda had already ordered a bottle of champagne. Their glasses were filled but untouched. "I'll just have a glass of their champagne."

"I'll have the same." Morgan returned the wine list to the waiter.

Glen cleared his throat and took Brenda's hand. "Maddie, Morgan, we wanted you both to be the first to know. Brenda has agreed to become my wife."

Maddie felt her eyes fill with tears. Tears of joy. Her father had learned to love again. There was no mistaking the love he had for Brenda, or the love she returned. Their feelings were in their smiles and in their eyes. "Oh, Dad, Brenda, I'm so happy for you both. Congratulations!"

"See, Brenda, I told you she'd be happy." Glen moved his chair closer to his fiancée.

Morgan nodded to the waiter, who had returned to the table with two champagne glasses. The waiter filled both glasses and added a few drops to Glen's and Brenda's. "Congratulations,

Glen and Brenda," Morgan said. "So when's the big day?"

"Wait a minute," Maddie exclaimed. "What did you mean by that last comment, Dad? Brenda, why didn't you think that I'd be happy?" She'd never done or said anything to lead anyone to that opinion. Actually, she hadn't said much at all about her father's and Brenda's growing relationship, mainly because she was scared of jinxing it.

"I didn't say you wouldn't be happy," Brenda explained. "I said I was concerned about how you would take the news. Your father and you have been alone for a long time. You might not appreciate another woman entering his life."

She relaxed in her chair. Was that all that was bothering Brenda? "I'm a little too old to be nervous about the Cinderella complex." She reached across the table and took Brenda's hands. "My only concern is for my father's happiness." She glanced at her father and grinned. "He looks extremely happy to me. So, I only have four words for you, Brenda. Welcome to the family."

Brenda released one of her hands and dabbed at her eyes with her linen napkin. "Oh, and I promised your father I wouldn't cry."

Glen wrapped his arm around Brenda's shoulders. "Now, Maddie, see what you've gone and done?"

She couldn't see anything past her own tears. She released Brenda's other hand and grabbed her own napkin. Blinking rapidly, she hoped to hold back her own tears, but all she managed to do was send the huge drops rolling down her cheeks. "I'm sorry, Dad." She dabbed delicately at her eyes. Her father would be lucky if she and Brenda didn't resemble a pair of raccoons by the night's end.

Glen looked totally bewildered by the crying women. His arms were full of his future wife, so he glared at Morgan and snapped, "Don't just sit there, Morgan, do something!"

The look of matching bewilderment on Morgan's face nearly did her in. They were attracting quite a lot of attention, but for once she didn't care. Her father was getting married! She felt Morgan's arm slip around her shoulders and she instinctively turned toward him.

He brushed her ear with his lips as he murmured, "Maddie, are you all right?"

She dabbed once more beneath her eyes and smiled up at him. All right? She was ecstatic! Nothing could have made her happier.

Morgan groaned as he studied her face. His fingers tightened against her shoulder as his gaze locked with hers. "My Lord, Maddie, you're even beautiful when you cry."

Two and a half hours later, Maddie unlocked her cottage door and practically danced across the threshold. Morgan was one step behind her, chuckling. "If I hadn't seen you drink only one glass of champagne, I would swear you were drunk."

She tossed her coat onto the couch and grinned at him. "Do you believe they set the wedding for Thanksgiving weekend? That's only five weeks away!"

"Brenda wants her son there, and with his teaching schedule it would either have to be Thanksgiving or Christmas break. It was your father who insisted he wasn't waiting for Christmas." Morgan loosened his tie and undid the top button of his shirt.

She felt as if she were floating on top of the world. Her father had found love again, and all evening Morgan had been plying her with compliments and devouring her with his intense gaze. She had a gut feeling tonight would be Morgan's "soon." What more could a woman possibly want? "Would you like me to put some coffee on?"

"No, thank you." He reached out and drew her into his arms.

"A horse! A horse! My kingdom for a horse!" screamed José.

"To be or not to be!" shrieked Manuel.

She lowered her forehead against Morgan's chest and felt his silent laughter vibrating through her. For a wild moment she had hoped he would kiss her and put an end to her torment. José and Manuel's timing definitely needed some improvement.

"I see you've been busy teaching them a better class of sayings to heckle me with."

"Shakespeare one-oh-one." She pulled back and smiled up at him. He didn't look too upset with her featherbrained pets. "It beats some of the limericks they know."

"Kiss me, Kate!" cried Manuel.

Morgan glanced over at the cage. "You got it wrong, Manuel." He pulled her in closer and lowered his mouth till it was nearly touching hers. "It's kiss me, Maddie."

"Kiss me, Maddie! Kiss me, Maddie!" repeated Manuel.

"Kiss a Wookiee! Kiss this! Kiss my—"

"José!" Maddie shouted as she pulled out of Morgan's arms. "Bad boy!"

José bobbed his head in agreement. "Bad boy, bad boy," he sang as he danced back and forth on his wooden perch.

Morgan turned away from the bird and chuckled, trying to cover it up with a cough. It had to be one of the worst pretend coughs Maddie had ever heard.

She couldn't blame him. She felt like giggling herself, but she knew that only encouraged the birds. "Yes, José, that was very bad." She walked over to his cage and waved her finger at the parrot. "It's bedtime for you both." She reached down into a box near the cages and picked up their jungle-print cage covers.

Here's Lookin' at You

She smiled at Manuel. "Good night, Manuel. You were a good boy."

"Kiss me, Kate, we will be married o' Sunday," cried Manuel as he made kissing sounds.

She chuckled as she slipped the cover over Manuel's cage. Turning to the other cage, she eyed José. "Say something nice, José."

"Nice!" José repeated.

She shook her head. José was incorrigible. "It's bedtime for you, my fine feathered friend."

"Lovers to bed; 'tis almost fairy time!" squawked José as she raised the cover for his cage. "Lovers to bed!"

Maddie felt a blush sweep up her face, but refused to turn around to look at Morgan. The man sounded like he was coughing to death. Whatever had possessed her to teach José that particular saying? She placed the cover over his cage, but before securing it, she whispered, "Good night, good night! Parting is such sweet sorrow."

José made a rude sound and said, "Bull!" as she closed the material.

She fussed around the cages for a minute, hoping the flush staining her cheeks would lessen before she faced Morgan. She was checking Manuel's cover for the second time when Morgan pulled her away from the cage and into his arms. She instinctively raised her mouth for his kiss, but was disappointed when he started to slow dance instead. All through dinner she'd been thinking about the wonderful kisses they had shared the previous night.

"I've been wanting to dance with you all evening, Maddie." His mouth brushed the top of her head. "But Brenda and Glen wanted to discuss the wedding, so I had to bide my time." Morgan's movements were slow and seductive. He danced like a lover. Hip to hip, chest to chest, they swayed in a tiny circle in the middle of her living room. "Dance with me now, sweet Maddie."

She followed his rhythm as smoothly as if they had danced together a thousand times. Pressing her cheek against his chest, she listened to the steady beat of his heart. The subtle scent of his aftershave enticed her senses. She wanted to get closer to his warmth. She wanted to pick up where they had left off the night before, but tonight she didn't want to stop. "Morgan?"

"Yes?"

As Yewanna Synne she felt seductive, feminine, and totally brazen. She could vamp any man who swaggered into the shire. With Morgan she felt hesitant, unsure, even scared. Something was happening to her, and it wasn't just a case of rioting hormones. Morgan had the power to make her feel and make her want more out of life. He made her want to believe that love had the power to be kind. She didn't want to be Yewanna Synne, she wanted to be herself for Morgan.

She pressed closer to him as his hands stroked her back. "Don't you think I should turn on some

Here's Lookin' at You

music?" She didn't mind dancing without music. The song "Some Enchanted Evening" was drifting through her mind. The only problem was, Morgan wasn't keeping time to that particular song.

"Who needs music when I have you in my arms?" He continued to sway to some unheard melody.

Oh, damn, he had gone and done it again. The man just opened his mouth and she went all soft and gooey inside. The rapid pounding of his heart beneath her ear matched her own. The dance was affecting him as much as it was touching her. She slipped her hands inside his suit jacket and ran her fingertips up his spine. She felt him tremble, and smiled. "What song are you dancing to, Morgan?"

" 'As Time Goes By.' " He wrapped one of her curls around his finger. "Do you realize that I've known you for your entire life?"

"I heard your parents brought you to my christening and that you demanded to know if your new baby brother or sister was going to cry as much as me. When your mother truthfully answered yes, you told her to take the baby out of her stomach and give it back. You didn't want all that racket at your house."

Morgan chuckled. "I don't remember that far back, but I do remember the time you and Georgia tried to have a tea party with my G.I. Joe men." His fingers lifted her chin so he could gaze at her face. "Who would have thought that pigtailed little girl with mischief in her green eyes would have turned out to be one very special woman?"

Maddie gazed into his dark eyes and couldn't think of one reason why they shouldn't become lovers. She wanted him, and his body betrayed his desire for her. It had been so long since a man had held her in his arms. So long since she had opened up and shared part of herself with a man.

Maybe there was something magical about the night, like José had said. She knew it was just a sentence she had taught him and José didn't even know what it meant, but it suited her mood perfectly. She reached up, stroked her thumb over Morgan's cheek, and smiled. "Lover's to bed; 'tis almost fairy time."

Morgan stopped dancing. "Are you saying what I think you're saying, sweet Maddie?"

She let her fingers toy with the ends of his hair that brushed the back of his neck. If he didn't kiss her soon, she was going to die. "Last night you promised me soon." She stretched up on her toes and nipped his lower lip. "Is this soon enough for you?"

He groaned deep in his throat, crushed her against his chest, and claimed her mouth in a kiss that should have tripped the Richter scales all the way out in California. Not only did the earth move beneath her feet, it completely disappeared.

In the back of her mind she realized Morgan

had swept her up off her feet and was carrying her into the bedroom, but it didn't really register. She was too busy falling deeper and deeper into the vortex of his kiss. Liquid heat churned low in her stomach and the tips of her breasts tightened into twin points of sensation.

Her feet touched the floor the same instant Morgan released her mouth. "Tell me now, sweet Maddie mine, if this isn't what you want." His mouth trailed moist kisses down her throat. "If we go any further, I won't be able to stop." He raised his head and searched her face.

The darkened room made it difficult for her to read his expression, but she could hear his breathing and feel the rapid pounding of his heart beneath the palm of her hand. The light spilling in from the hallway and living room beyond cast a seductive glow across the bed. A glow she wanted to share with Morgan. She grabbed his tie and pulled his head back down to hers. "Make love with me, Morgan." She playfully bit his chin. "And if you dare stop, I'll sic José and Manuel on you."

Morgan returned her playful nip with one of his own. "Threats, Slim?"

"Promises." This time she gave his tie a harder yank and captured his mouth as his head lowered. The vortex once again swirled around her as he deepened the kiss with a bold thrust of his tongue.

Morgan felt Maddie's tongue wrap around his

and nearly died from her sweetness. Her hand still had its stranglehold on his tie, but he didn't care. If he died right that second, he would die a happy man. Well, almost. He hoped the grim reaper would hold off for a couple more hours. He wanted to make love to Maddie just once before he met his Maker. He wanted that memory with him for eternity.

He shuddered as she released his tie and pushed his suit jacket off his shoulders. Without releasing her mouth, he shrugged to help her. The Italian-made jacket landed on the floor with barely a sound. His hands immediately went back to holding Maddie. Learning Maddie. And by the soft little purrs emerging from her throat, pleasing Maddie. He cupped her hips and brought her in closer contact with his aching arousal.

She pulled her mouth away from his and gulped in some air. "Please, Morgan," she begged.

"Please what?" He knew what she wanted; it was gleaming in her green Irish eyes. He wanted to hear the words, though, needed to hear the words.

Soft lips skimmed his jaw and delicate fingers went to work on the buttons of his shirt. "You know what."

His fingernail ran down the zipper in the back of her dress, but he didn't undo it. They had all night to tease and tempt each other, and he planned on using every minute of it. He lowered

Here's Lookin' at You

his mouth to the enticing soft spot below her ear and felt her tremble. "Tell me what you want."

His shirt was brushed off his shoulders. Maddie muttered a curse as his sleeves got stuck. "Damn." She had forgotten to undo the buttons on his cuffs.

He chuckled. She seemed so disgusted with herself. "I'm beginning to think that maybe you don't have a lot of practice in taking off men's shirts."

She stopped her struggle with the left cuff and looked up at him. "Are you going to help me or what?"

"You haven't told me what you want yet." He was so hard, he was afraid to touch her for fear of losing what little control he had left.

He didn't like the way Maddie squinted her eyes at him. She had done that on one or two occasions in the past, and it usually meant she was thinking about something he might not agree with. "Now, Maddie . . ." He lost the words he was about to speak when she smiled. It wasn't a nice smile, or even a friendly smile. It was a smile that said she was the cat and he had just turned into a canary. It was a seductive, feminine smile that men had been avoiding and praying for all their lives.

Maddie seemed to growl before lowering her gaze to his bare chest and pressing her sweet, hot mouth directly over his thundering heart. Fire shot through his body as her lips seared his skin.

He nearly took a step back from the shock as she nipped at one of his nipples and sucked it in between her lips. He didn't think it was possible to take this slow and easy any longer. He hadn't been expecting this much heat. He should have known better. With Maddie he never knew what to expect.

Her mouth repeated the torturous pleasure to his other nipple before blazing lower. "I want you, Morgan." Her tongue circled his navel, before giving it a quick stab.

His stomach clenched and the ache of his arousal grew painful. Maddie's mouth was driving him over the edge. He reached for her shoulders and hauled her back up to his mouth. He had his words, now he wanted the rest.

He reached for the zipper in the back of her dress, but came up short. His damn shirt was balled around his elbows, restricting his movements. With a muttered curse he released her mouth, unfastened his right cuff, and pulled his arm out of the sleeve.

Maddie smiled as her fingers danced across his belt buckle. "Careful, or I might get the impression that you don't have a lot of practice in taking off women's dresses."

He growled at the other cuff as he finally released the button and the shirt landed on top of his jacket. "I don't." He reached for her zipper again, and this time the brass fastening slid all the way down her spine to the small of her back. With

Here's Lookin' at You

slow movements he brushed the black dress over her shoulders and down her arms. The snappy dress, which had been driving him crazy all night, pooled around her feet.

Maddie undid his buckle and ran her fingernail down his bulging zipper. "You did that pretty well for a man who'd just claimed not to have a lot of experience."

He shuddered and captured her wandering hand. "Now I know where José and Manuel get it from." His gaze slowly traveled the length of her body. She was more beautiful than he had dreamed. Luscious breasts overfilled the lacy black cups of her bra. Berry-hard nipples poked against the lace, threatening the diaphanous material. A flimsy scrap of black lace barely classified itself as panties. But what fascinated him were the black satin garter belt and the silky black stockings attached to it.

He knew about garter belts and stockings, but he'd never actually seen a pair on a woman before. The pale skin between the top of her black stockings and the lacy edge of her panties looked creamy and sweet. The person who had invented pantyhose should be shot. His mouth was bone dry, yet he felt as if he was about to embarrass himself by drooling.

When he spoke, his voice was uneven and harsh, even to his own ears. "You wore this to the country club?" If he had known that, he never would have made it through dinner.

Maddie seemed to enjoy his discomfort. "I hate pantyhose." She kicked off her shoes and immediately lost two inches in height. Her fingers wove through the dark hair on his chest and playfully pulled. "I've been trying to work up my nerve to ask you something."

"What?" He kicked off his shoes, but couldn't manage his socks. His hands went to the waistband of his slacks, but froze in the process of unsnapping them. Playful and seductive Maddie suddenly looked lost. He reached out and cupped her cheek. "What is it, Slim?"

"Do you have . . . ummm . . . you know?" She blushed a brilliant scarlet, which even in the shadowy room he could detect.

"Do I have what?" Lord, was she trying to ask if he had anything that was contagious? "I'm in perfect health, if that's your question."

She shook her head and, amazingly, blushed more. "No, Morgan. I'm not in the habit of"—she nodded toward the bed—"this. I'm not prepared."

He relaxed and gave a silent sigh. For a moment there, she had really worried him. He swung her up in his arms and lowered her to the bed. His mouth trailed down her throat to the valley between her breasts. She had applied perfume there, the scent of lavender strong among the soft curves. He raised his head and straightened back up. "Yes, Slim, I have something."

He groaned as she stretched like a cat and grinned. "Good," she murmured.

He stood at the bottom of the bed and quickly finished undressing. Maddie was a paradox, an enticing paradox. She was stretched out on her bed like a seductive goddess, yet she blushed like an innocent when questioning him about birth control. He reached into his pants pocket and found what she had requested. When confronted with a puzzle at work, he always found it best to start at the bottom and work his way up. He glanced at Maddie's long, shapely legs outlined by black nylons and felt his heart drop to his knees. He'd never had a puzzle with such a beguiling bottom before.

Maddie felt Morgan's fingers slowly stroke up her leg and gripped the chenille bedspread with her fists. Heat blazed where his fingers touched. She closed her eyes and allowed the sensations to wash over her. Liquid want seeped from her abdomen and pooled between her thighs. Morgan was doing the most delicious things to her body, and he had barely touched her. Her nipples were desperate for his touch, and as for the secret womanly place guarded by a pair of black panties, it was moist with need. She was ready and aching for him.

His mouth brushing the top of her thigh sent her eyes wide open with shock. Sweet shock. Her hands released the bedspread and reached for him as a soft plea tumbled from her lips. "Morgan."

Warm lips skimmed her abdomen as hot fingers undid the tabs of her garters. Morgan's gaze seemed to burn into hers as he whispered, "Soon, sweet Maddie of mine."

She tugged at his shoulders as the other stocking came undone. "Now, Morgan."

He grazed another kiss across her stomach as he pulled her panties and garter belt over her hips and down her legs. His fingers stroked down her legs and then slowly back up. He didn't miss an inch. "Soon," he whispered against her belly as his hands skimmed higher.

Maddie thought she'd go out of her mind. She reached for him, but he expertly kept the majority of his body out of her reach. Frustration mounted along with her desire. She wanted Morgan, and she wanted him now. She tried to sit up, only to have him unclasp her bra and peel the clinging lace away with his teeth. He gazed down at her exposed breasts, whispered one word—"Beautiful"—then pulled one of her nipples deep into his mouth.

She arched her hips off the bed and pressed his mouth closer. Lord, she had never felt like this before. The heat was unbearable, the emptiness agonizing, and the need to have Morgan fill that void was above all else.

She forced his mouth up to hers. Her thighs naturally parted and her legs wrapped around his hips. The slick, smooth skin of his back felt feverish hot beneath her touch. "Now, Morgan, now."

She could feel his arousal nudging her inner thigh, and arched her hips higher.

Strong, tender hands cupped her face and forced her to look at him. "Are you ready for me, Maddie?"

The nylon-clad heel of her foot dug into the back of his thigh. "I've been ready." She felt him adjust his weight and gently nudge at the dewy opening between her legs. Her eyes closed as he slowly started to fill the emptiness.

He stopped. "Open your eyes, Maddie. I want to see your soul."

She opened her eyes and looked straight up into his probing stare. Her breathing was wild and erratic as he pushed deeper, but she didn't break the contact.

"Do you want me, Maddie?"

"Yes," she moaned. Morgan looked to be in pain. His jaw was clenched and sweat coated his brow.

Between clamped teeth he asked, "Do you need me?"

She could feel him sink deeper and ran her hand down his back and onto his muscle-clenched buttocks. "Yes." She could tell he was using every ounce of strength he had to go slow. But why? She didn't want him slow and easy. She wanted the ache to go away.

His fingers trembled against her flushed cheeks. "Do you love me?"

Her breath lodged in her throat as she stared

at him. Did she love Morgan? *Yes.* Did she want to love Morgan? *No.* She didn't want to love any man, but she had gone and done it anyway. Lying to Morgan was not an option. He could see her soul and would know it was a lie. On a breathless sigh she gave him his answer. "Yes."

He dropped his mouth to hers and murmured, "Thank you," then filled her with one powerful thrust.

Maddie's world suddenly tilted. She grasped at Morgan and held on tight. It was all she could do. The ride had begun and she wasn't in control. She didn't know how to control the feelings flooding her body. She matched Morgan thrust for thrust, moan for moan. The sound of their heavy breathing filled the room.

She went upward with each thrust. Skyward to a place she had never been before. A place that had no boundaries, no edge. A place that contained only Morgan. A place that was beginning to scare her even while it compelled her to reach further.

"Come with me, sweet Maddie." Morgan pulled back and almost completely left her. "Hang on, love, I've got you."

She wrapped her arms tighter around him and hung on. With his next powerful thrust he pushed them both spiraling out of control. She closed her eyes and allowed the place to claim her. In the distance she could hear Morgan chanting her name as he reached his climax, and she knew she was safe.

Morgan continued to hold her securely in his arms as her breathing slowed to its regular rhythm. She was semi-awake when she felt him roll her stockings down her legs and pull the covers out from underneath her and over her. His body was warm as it joined her between the sheets.

A gentle kiss brushed her forehead. "Lovers to bed," Morgan said as he nestled her against him.

She smiled sleepily and answered, " 'Tis almost fairy time."

NINE

Morgan watched as Maddie escorted the last of Glen and Brenda's engagement party guests to the front hall. The woman had been driving him wild all night. Twice he had managed to catch her in a secluded corner and steal a few kisses, but they had only fanned his frustration. In the past two weeks, since they had become lovers, his desire for Maddie had only increased. It hadn't mattered that he had spent every night in her bed. He wanted her more today than yesterday. His instincts and heart were telling him he would never get enough of Maddie. His instincts and heart were also telling him something wasn't right.

In the bright light of day, Maddie held something of herself back. He could not only feel it, he could see it in her eyes. Sometimes he glimpsed what he thought was fear and it tore at his heart. What was she afraid of? Being hurt was the only answer he could come up with. He would rather rip out his own heart than break hers.

He loved her.

Under the cover of darkness and in the heat of passion, Maddie held nothing back. She was wild, wonderful, and entirely his. She never freely admitted to loving him, but when he brought her to the edge of fulfillment and demanded to know if she did or not, she always confessed her love. The tactic of extorting an answer from her didn't sit well with him, but he was desperate. He needed to know what she was feeling. He couldn't possibly be the only one experiencing the roller-coaster emotion of love.

He wanted a future with Maddie and he was prepared to fight whatever demons were tearing at her soul in order to get it.

Maddie had sworn she had never suffered a broken heart, yet that day in her father's study she had seemed upset about the very idea of getting married, and children appeared to be out of the question. But why?

The day her father had been released from the hospital, he had stopped by to see if they needed any help. He had accompanied Maddie to the pediatric ward to deliver the dozen or so balloons Glen had received, along with half a dozen flower arrangements. Maddie's heartfelt concern for the children had been obvious.

Glen had also told him the other week that Maddie had never stayed in the waiting area while he suffered through his therapy sessions. She went down to the pediatric ward and read books to the children. Morgan knew for a fact that her visits hadn't stopped. A few days earlier he had found a bag full of new children's books in her bedroom closet.

Maddie was going to make a wonderful wife and mother, just as soon as he convinced her to take a chance on him and their future. He had hinted around the subject the other day just to see what her reaction might be. He had never seen someone change the topic so fast.

Morgan glanced around the room and headed for the baby grand piano, artfully arranged in front of one of the patio doors leading to the gardens beyond. Glen had hired a pianist to entertain the guests, and the light melodies that had floated through the house all evening had set the mood perfectly.

But there was one song he wanted to hear, "As Time Goes By."

Morgan pulled out the shiny black bench and sat. The upright piano at his house wasn't quite so extravagant, but it played the same clear notes. When he was a boy he had hated his parents' insistence that he learn to play. As he grew older he skipped from classical to rock and roll and impressed quite a few girls with his talent. He still played the piano, but he didn't do it to impress anyone. He did it for his love of music.

He started to play "As Time Goes By" the

same instant Maddie stepped back into the room. She looked sexy as all hell heading his way carrying two glasses of champagne. The emerald silk dress she wore fit her as if it had been custom made to drive him out of his mind. It was a good thing he had met her at her father's just after the party started, or they never would have made it out of her cottage. The shimmering dress was sleeveless, backless, and totally bewitching. It ended above her shapely knees and she had on stockings with a back seam. That could mean only one thing, that she was once again wearing the sexy garter belt that had so aroused him the first time they made love. Her hair was pinned up into a sophisticated style that made his fingers itch to pull every last pin out of it. Emerald stud earrings and a matching necklace completed the outfit.

With her red hair and green eyes, Maddie was an emerald person. He wanted to drape her in emeralds and nothing else.

He smiled but didn't stop playing as she set the two glasses on the piano. " 'Of all the gin joints in all the towns in all the world, she walks into mine.' "

Maddie returned his smile. "You got it all wrong. Bogey didn't play the piano in *Casablanca*, Sam did."

As the song came to an end he immediately went into another number from the classic movie, "It Had To Be You." "I stand corrected." He moved over a couple of inches. "Sit down. You've been on your feet all night."

She sat and leaned her head against his shoulder. "I can still remember listening to you practice for hours when you were young."

"If I remember correctly, you took lessons too." He nudged her shoulder with his. "Join me?"

She chuckled. "I only know two songs. 'Chopsticks' and the easy portion of that all-time duet favorite, 'Heart and Soul.' "

He finished "It Had To Be You" and nuzzled her neck. He liked the enticing view of her neck with her hair all swept up like that. "I know another popular duet we could do together." His lips found her rapid pulse in the hollow of her throat, and he knew she understood what he had been talking about.

"Dad and Brenda are saying good-bye to her son, Cliff, and his wife."

"I wasn't really thinking about doing that particular duet on your father's piano." He nibbled her earlobe. "But if you're having some type of fantasy involving a piano, we could always go to my place." He swept his tongue over the area he had just been nibbling on. "Of course, it's not a baby grand, but if I remove the pictures and the other stuff, I'm sure we could manage without breaking anything important. Like an arm or a leg."

She seductively trailed her fingers up his thigh.

"Gee, Morgan, you really know how to sweep a girl off her feet."

He captured her fingers before they went any higher. "Hey, it isn't me with the musical fantasy." Glen and Brenda were going to walk back into the room at any moment and he didn't want to embarrass himself or Maddie. He was pretty sure Glen knew what was happening between them, but he wasn't about to put it on public display. He made a point of leaving Maddie's cottage around dawn, before Glen usually awoke.

He wasn't against a shotgun wedding, but he much preferred to win Maddie's love and acceptance the old-fashioned way.

He raised her fingers to his lips and pressed a kiss onto each one. His body hardened at the look that leaped into her eyes. "Can we leave now," he asked, "or is there something else you need to do?" If he didn't get her out of there within the next few minutes, he would be locking the door and making love to her on top of the piano.

"The caterers are finishing up in the kitchen. There's nothing left for me to do but to say good night to my father and Brenda."

Morgan stood and reached for her hand. "Let's go say good night."

Maddie had just stood when Glen and Brenda entered the room. Both looked radiantly happy. "Are you two leaving already?" Glen asked.

"It's after one, Dad." Maddie kissed her father's cheek. "Good night. I'll see you tomorrow." She turned to Brenda. "I think the party turned out wonderfully. Both your son and daughter seemed to have enjoyed themselves."

Brenda beamed. "They did. I'm so glad this party is over with. Now I can concentrate on putting the final arrangements on the ceremony and reception." Brenda clasped Maddie's hand. "I couldn't have done it without you, Maddie. You've been such a help."

"It's been fun, Brenda. You don't have to thank me."

"It's good experience for when she plans her own wedding," Glen said, and gave Morgan a meaningful look.

Morgan could see Maddie's embarrassment and felt her pain. Glen looked quite pleased with himself for that snappy little remark, but Morgan wished the older man had kept his mouth shut. Maddie wasn't a woman you could push into anything. The more you pushed, the harder she stood her ground.

Morgan shook Glen's hand. "It was a great party, Glen." He smiled, but could feel the strain behind it. Glen seemed oblivious to his tension and Maddie's pain. Her father had hurt her, and he hadn't even noticed. He had once thought Glen was as close to perfect as a human being could get, now he knew better. Glen was simply human.

Morgan kissed Brenda's cheek. At least she seemed to sense the tension and was baffled by it.

After Maddie had gotten her coat, they headed for her cottage through the garden, taking the fastest path. He needed to get her mind off what her father had said and onto something more pleasurable. He knew exactly how to distract Maddie, but he needed the privacy of her cottage to do it.

They entered by the kitchen door. Morgan locked the door, then prevented Maddie from turning on the lights. The soft glow from the lamp she'd left on in the living room gave him enough light to see by.

"Morgan, what are you doing?" Maddie slipped off her coat and draped it over the back of one of the chairs.

The red roses he had given her a few days earlier sat in the center of the kitchen table. He put them on the counter, out of harm's way. "Your fantasy about the piano has given me an idea of my own." He took off his suit jacket and tie and draped them over another chair before pulling her into his arms.

She kicked off her high heels and lifted her mouth for his kiss. "I never had a fantasy about the piano, Morgan. It was your perverted mind that conjured up that one."

He arched a brow at her wicked smile. "You might be right on that one, love." He eyed the red Formica table with a great deal of interest. "What's your opinion on kitchen tables?"

"They're perfect for serving a meal on, Morgan, but not for what you're thinking." She glanced at the table with a combination of horror and speculation.

Noting her expression, he burst out laughing. He had her, and he knew he had her. Some tiny part of Maddie was at least intrigued. He picked her up and set her on the table.

She let out a squeal as her feet left the ground. "Morgan!"

He smiled against her throat. "Prepare to be ravished, Slim."

"Ravished!" She tilted her head and gave him better access to her neck. "I've never been ravished before." He could feel her hands stroking his back, pulling him nearer. "Will I like it?"

His fingers made fast work of the zipper of her dress. "Trust me, Slim," he said as he pushed the green silk straps down her arms. "You're going to love it."

Half an hour later, Maddie cuddled against his side in her bed. The table was great for some things, but it wasn't built for comfort. He pulled her closer and kissed the top of her head. She was being awfully quiet. "So, Slim, what did you think about your first ravishment?"

Her fingers toyed with the hair on his chest. "You did that very well, Morgan. Were you a pirate in a previous life?"

"The closest I came to ever being a pirate was

when Manuel screamed at me to walk the plank." He stroked the lush indentation of her waist and the flare of her hips. "Does that count?"

"Hardly." Her pensive sigh tore at his heart. Something was upsetting her, but what? "Morgan?"

"Hmmm . . ." It had to be what her father had said before they left his house. Everything had been going so well before then.

"You're not taking what my father said seriously, are you?"

He was right. Glen's words were upsetting her. He didn't agree with Glen with coming right out and saying it, but he wasn't about to pretend they hadn't meant anything to him. "Your father's a very levelheaded man, Slim. At times he has some brilliant ideas."

"It's his own pending marriage that made him say that, Morgan. In his happiness with Brenda, he feels the whole damn world would be a better place if everyone was married."

"Well, I don't know about the whole world, Maddie. But—" His words were cut off so fast he nearly fell out of bed from the whiplash.

"Did I tell you the Dutch Apple Theater called today?" Maddie's voice was breathless. "They want me back for another audition. I definitely have a job there, but they aren't sure which role I'll be cast in."

He let the subject of marriage and their future drop. If she wasn't in the mood to even discuss it, there was no way in hell she would accept his proposal. It looked like he was destined to wait longer. The only problem was, the waiting was becoming harder and harder.

He gave her a hug. "That's great, love. Which parts are you up for and how can I get a ticket for every one of your performances?"

Maddie glanced around the White Lace and Promises Bridal Boutique with a sense of amazement. Cleo, the owner, was fussing over Brenda as if she were visiting royalty. Two other assistants were bustling around Sarah, Brenda's daughter, and Alyssa, her granddaughter. Another assistant was busy pulling every dark green dress they had in the boutique onto a rack in front of her for her inspection. Her father and Brenda had decided on a small private ceremony in her church with a luncheon reception to follow at the country club. No fewer than a hundred people had been invited. Obviously her father and Brenda's idea of small and private wasn't hers.

Brenda had decided on a cream-colored suit with intricate beadwork detailing the front of the jacket. Sarah had picked a lovely knee-length dress in maroon. Alyssa was being measured for her dress, which combined all three colors—cream, maroon, and dark green—in a wonderful print.

Maddie studied the dozen or so dresses hanging on the rack. Six she dismissed outright. Two were maybes, but the rest were wonderful. She couldn't find a darn thing wrong with any of them. So why wasn't she dashing off to the dressing room to try them on? What was wrong with her?

She glanced again at the mannequin dominating the front window. She had been perfectly fine and happy until she had seen that mannequin, or to be more precise, that dress. The white satin wedding gown was exquisite. There had to be a hundred thousand pearly white beads hand sewn onto the gown. Yards of white lace flowed flawlessly, and the satin, lace, and beaded train was at least six yards long. And the veil! You would probably have to show your birth certificate to prove you were indeed a fairy-tale princess and allowed to wear such a gorgeous headpiece. The dress, the veil, and even the silk bouquet of white roses were every girl's fantasy as to what a bride should be. They had been hers.

Maddie turned away from the display and stared unseeingly at the dress in front of her. What did it matter now that when she was ten she'd had four different wedding gowns for her Barbies? She wasn't ten any longer and she wasn't getting married. She blinked back a pair of tears and concentrated on the gowns.

She didn't understand her own moods lately. Maybe it was all the strain she had been under. First there was her father's stroke, then his recovery. Then her father's announcement that she would become president of the quarries if something happened to him and his express desire to have grandchildren. Then Morgan entered her life and turned it completely upside down. Her father and Brenda's engagement and their desire for a quick wedding hadn't helped matters, along with her father's embarrassing matchmaking attempts.

Weddings had been occupying a lot of her time lately. It hadn't helped that the night before, Morgan and she had been invited to Georgia and her new husband's house for dinner. It had been a long time since she had seen Georgia, but there had been no mistaking her happiness and the love she felt for her husband.

Everywhere around her, people were in love and getting married. Didn't they realize what could happen? Didn't her father realize that Brenda could die and he would once again be seeing the world through the bottom of a whiskey bottle, and maybe this time he wouldn't be able to climb back out? Did Brenda really want to take a chance on becoming a widow again? What about Georgia? She knew how hard Georgia's parents' deaths had been on her. What was going to happen to her if her new husband died? She couldn't imagine the devastation her friend would feel. She didn't want to imagine it.

Love belonged only in a perfect world. In a perfect world people didn't die.

"Did you find something, Maddie?" Brenda asked as she looked over Maddie's shoulder. "Oh, that one's beautiful. Quick, go try it on. I want to see."

Maddie braced herself for the performance of a lifetime. She would rather jump in front of a train than ruin Brenda and her father's wedding. She reached for the hanger and pulled the dress off the rack, thankful it was one of the "wonderful" ones, and headed for the dressing room. "I'll be right out."

By the time Maddie had tried on the fourth dress, she knew the first dress she'd had on was the one. She stood in front of the mirror and glanced at Brenda's and Sarah's reflections. "Definitely the first one I had on."

Brenda and her daughter nodded in agreement. "You look beautiful in all of them, Maddie. But there was something about the first one that just suited you best."

"I can't imagine her looking more beautiful," drawled Morgan, who had entered the shop with her father and Sarah's husband and son.

Maddie felt herself flush as she met his gaze in the mirror. The men had been at a tuxedo shop a couple of streets over. The agreement had been for them all to meet at the boutique, then the entire bridal party was going out to lunch. She hadn't been shocked three weeks earlier when her father asked Morgan to be his best man, just a tad anxious. She didn't want to be standing anywhere near a church altar with Morgan and a preacher. Her gaze focused in on the mannequin, directly behind Morgan. In the light of the early afternoon sun the mannequin appeared to have red hair.

Morgan turned his head and followed her gaze.

Maddie sat in the passenger seat of Morgan's car and stared at her cottage. "Really, Morgan, you didn't have to drive me home. My father was going to."

"It isn't a problem. Your place was on the way back to my office anyway." Morgan turned off the ignition and faced her. "Is something bothering you, Maddie? You were awfully quiet all through lunch."

She tried to smile, but it slipped a little around the edges. "I've had a lot on my mind lately, that's all."

"Us?"

She looked away from his questioning dark eyes. Questions she didn't want to examine, let alone answer. She had been on the verge of tears all day. Tears she didn't understand. "Look, Morgan, I've got to get going. I'm due at the theater in an hour."

"I'll let you go this time, Maddie. But we are going to have that conversation soon, real soon."

She opened the car door and ran into the cottage as if the hounds of hell were after her. Morgan's "soons" had a way of happening real fast.

Morgan paced Maddie's living room and listened to the shower running in the bathroom. Yesterday he would have joined her under the pounding spray and scrubbed her back or any other place she might have wanted rubbed. But not tonight. Tonight he was going to ask Maddie to become his wife. He'd never considered himself a masochist, but he might well be one.

He had been in his office going over a major bid his firm was about to submit when he'd realized he couldn't take any more. Well, it hadn't happened quite like that. Ben, De Witt Asphalt's purchasing agent, had barged into his office and shoved a cigar in his hand. After six years of trying, Ben was about to become a father. Morgan had accepted the news with a grin and a handshake, and a promise of celebrating later. But after Ben had left and closed the door, he'd felt the ache. It started in his heart and spread outward. He wanted Maddie, and the happiness, and the children that would surely follow their union. And he wanted it now. He was thirty-eight years old and he wasn't getting any younger.

The sound of the shower being turned off made him pace faster. He had called Maddie from work and suggested dinner out, somewhere fancy and nice. She had pleaded exhaustion from rehearsing all day and countered with steaks on the grill and baked potatoes.

Maddie had been late getting home, and by the time she'd walked through the door, he had dinner ready. It had been a quiet meal. He had been the one to suggest she take a shower. He didn't want her falling asleep before he could "pop the question." Maddie hadn't been sleeping very well the past couple of nights. She tossed and turned for endless hours and the fatigue was beginning to show.

"Did you pick a movie?" she asked as she walked into the room, tying the belt on her robe. Her hideous robe.

He stopped by the box of videotapes and only then remembered he was supposed to have picked one out while she showered. He dropped onto her couch and patted the seat next to him. "Sit down, Maddie. You look exhausted." The dark shadows under her eyes were more pronounced now that her makeup had been washed away.

She sat and curled her feet up under herself. "What happened to all that charm you used to have?"

He could tell her smile was meant to soften her words, but it hadn't. "I say screw the charm when the woman I love is beating herself into the ground." He tenderly stroked his thumb over the shadows under her eyes. "Tell me what's wrong, Slim."

"Nothing is wrong, Morgan. I'm just a little

tired, that's all." She captured his hand and gave it a squeeze. "A nice relaxing evening at home is what I need. The shower did wonders, and if you hurry up and pick a movie, I just might stay awake for the whole thing."

He was afraid he wasn't going to be giving her that relaxing evening. He didn't want to admit it, but it was their relationship that was causing her so much anxiety. The next step had to be taken, for she couldn't go on like this. Neither could he. "Can I ask you a question, Slim?"

She covered a yawn with her hand before replying, "Shoot."

He took a deep breath and blurted, "Will you marry me?"

Maddie blinked twice. "No."

He stiffened at her blunt refusal, but resisted being heartbroken. He'd known she would say no. Now it was time to find out why. "Why not?"

"I'm an actress, Morgan."

"What's that got to do with marrying me? You've been an actress for ten years. I don't expect you to change for me. I love you just the way you are. There are plenty of places within Lancaster County for your talents, and if you have to go farther afield, I'm sure we can work something out."

She twisted her hands together in her lap and continued to blink her eyes. He could see the tears filling those eyes faster than she could blink. "There are some highly influential people in the

Here's Lookin' at You

county who would be scandalized if you marry an actress. My father's business suffered when he married my mother."

"That was thirty-five years ago, Maddie. Think up another excuse, because that one wasn't worth your breath or my time to respond to it." She was grasping at straws, he could see it. Why wouldn't she at least give him the truth? She loved him, he knew that in the depth of his heart, so why? He had one final card left to play. His trump card. He had been hoping he wouldn't need it, but he wasn't afraid to use it if he had to. It looked like he had to.

"Morgan, I don't think—"

"I'll give you something to think about, Maddie. Think how happy it would make your father to see you get married." He covered her trembling hands with his own. "And imagine his joy when he learns you're pregnant with our first child."

She yanked her hands out from under his just as the tears overflowed her eyes and streamed down her face. She got to her feet and clutched the lapels of her robe together. "I told you I won't marry you, Morgan." She turned from him, but didn't wipe her tears away. "I think you should leave now."

He jumped to his feet. "Leave! You want me to leave, just like that!" He snapped his fingers. His trump card had failed. Her tears were ripping at his heart, but he really couldn't feel it. His heart was too busy breaking. "Tell me why, Maddie. Just tell me, why won't you take a chance on our future?"

"Future!" Her voice rose and her tears continued to fall. "How do you know there is a future? How can you be so damn certain?"

He stared at her for a long moment. "Your hair is damp, you have dark circles under your eyes, and you're crying, yet you're the most beautiful woman I have ever seen. Even that hideous bedspread you call a robe looks sexy to me." He ran his fingers through his hair. The words were coming out all wrong, but he didn't know how else to say them. "I pictured you a hundred times sitting in a rocking chair with the morning sun streaming in behind you. Your hair's a fiery halo around your shoulders, and that robe looks soft and warm against your body. Do you know what you're doing in my dreams, Maddie?"

She bit her lower lip and shook her head.

He picked up his jacket, which he'd thrown over the arm of the couch. "You're singing a lullaby and nursing our child." He saw the pain on her face, but he didn't stay. He couldn't stay. He had wanted forever, while Maddie wanted . . . He wasn't sure what Maddie had wanted.

He softly closed the cottage door behind him.

TEN

Morgan parked his car in front of Glen's house and stared at it through the windshield. Had it really been only a little over two months since he'd stopped by to make sure Maddie was settled in after her drive from Connecticut? He had to marvel at how much had changed in his life, and how much it had stayed the same. He was still alone and his house still echoed with emptiness, but sometimes late at night, if he listened real close, he could hear his own heart cry.

It had been four days since he asked Maddie to marry him and she had refused. Four days since he'd heard her voice, besides the message on her answering machine, seen her smile, or felt her touch. It had been four days of pure hell and he had nothing to look forward to except more of the same. Agonizing days and endless nights.

With a weary sigh he got out of the car and

headed up the path. Glen had called him earlier and requested that he stop by on his way home from work. He hadn't been giving Glen's request much thought because he figured it had to do with the wedding. The big event was eight days away. Eight more days before he would see Maddie again. There was no way Maddie would miss her own father's wedding. She couldn't avoid him forever. Sooner or later she was going to have to tell him the real reason she wouldn't marry him.

He knocked on the door and remembered the first time he had stopped by when Maddie was there and José and Manuel had invited him in. He even missed her parrots and their smart-aleck comments and being called hamster brain.

He had tried everything he could think of to get Maddie to at least talk to him. He sent flowers daily, both to her cottage and to the theater. She never answered her phone and twice he had stopped at the cottage, but both times her van hadn't been there and the lights were off. Yesterday he'd had a delivery boy hand deliver to the theater a black iron doorstop that was a replica of the Maltese Falcon. The day before that he sent a collection of Bogart videos with a note attached to *To Have and Have Not*, Bogey's first movie with the love of his life, Lauren Bacall. The note said, *If you ever need anything, just whistle. You remember how to whistle, don't you? Just put your lips together and blow.* Maddie never whistled.

Glen opened the door and frowned at him.

Here's Lookin' at You

"Come in, Morgan." Glen stepped back and allowed him to enter. "In my study, please."

Morgan knew something was up, something he wasn't going to like. Only on rare occasions did Glen insist on using his study. Morgan followed the older man, deeming it wise not to say anything until Glen told him what this was all about.

Glen sat behind his desk and waved to one of the leather wing chairs positioned in front of him. "Please sit, Morgan."

He sat in the same chair he had the last time he'd been called to this room. The day Glen informed Maddie he wanted grandchildren. Glen looked worse now than he did then. "Out with it, Glen. You know stress isn't good for you, and by the looks of things I'd say you're under a great deal right at this moment." He didn't know why he was being "called on the carpet," so to speak, but this anxiety wasn't doing Glen any good. The last thing he wanted was for Glen to suffer another stroke.

Glen took a deep breath, glared at him, and demanded, "Why did you break my daughter's heart?"

He sat there for a full minute letting Glen's words sink in. Glen actually thought Maddie was the one suffering a broken heart! How did life just keep getting better and better? "I don't know how I could have broken Maddie's heart, Glen. As far as I know, broken hearts don't come from marriage proposals and talk of babies."

Morgan watched in bitter amusement as Glen grappled with his words. He could practically see the words churning over in Glen's mind and the exact instant they finally registered. Glen's mouth opened and closed twice before he finally thundered, "Marriage! You asked Maddie to marry you?" Glen stood up and hurried around his desk, grabbed his hand, and pumped it up and down. "Welcome to the family, son! And you did say babies, didn't you, Morgan? Grandchildren! I'm going to be a grandfather!"

Morgan felt like a heel. Glen thought his wish was finally coming true, and Morgan was going to have to burst his bubble. He pulled his hand out of Glen's grasp. "Sit down, Glen, please."

Glen beamed and sat in the chair next to Morgan. "You're going to be my son-in-law. Well, I'll be damned."

"No, it's me who's going to be damned, Glen." He couldn't prevent the sigh that escaped him, but at least now he had Glen's full attention. "Yes, I did ask your daughter to marry me, and I even mentioned the possibility of children."

Glen frowned. "What happened?"

"Maddie turned me down flat. She even tossed my sorry butt out of her cottage." He lowered his head and studied his clasped hands, which were dangling between his knees. He didn't want to face Glen. "She won't even take my phone calls now." He heard his voice crack. His voice hadn't cracked when Helen had refused his proposal and

Here's Lookin' at You

admitted to loving another. His heart hadn't cried silently in the night either.

Glen was quiet for a moment. "Does she know you love her?"

"Yes, and she even loves me." It felt a little strange talking to Glen about his daughter. Glen was a friend, a good friend, but he was also Maddie's father. "I wasn't trifling with her heart if that's what you've been thinking."

"I've never known you to trifle with any woman, Morgan. I was thrilled when you two started seeing each other. I had hopes of welcoming you into the family." Glen drummed his fingers on the arm of the chair and then started to chuckle.

"What's so damn funny?" He couldn't believe it. Glen was laughing!

"The way history repeats itself." Glen laughed louder. "Relax, son. Maddie's only being stubborn, just like her mother."

"Stubborn?"

"I'll let you in on a secret, one Maddie doesn't even know about. Carolyn turned me down the first, second, and third times I asked her to marry me."

"You're kidding?"

"Nope." Glen shook his head, smiling at some distant memory. "If anyone knows how much alike Maddie and Carolyn are, it's me." Glen nodded. "Stands to reason that Maddie would turn you down too." He grinned at Morgan. "Don't worry, son. There'll be a wedding and plenty of babies. What do you think? Is four too many?"

For the first time in days, Morgan smiled. Maybe Glen was right. If anyone understood Maddie, it was her father. He knew her red hair was a bad sign, but he'd take her stubbornness as long as he got to love her for the rest of their lives. "Four babies? It has a nice ring to it, Glen. What do you think, two boys and two girls?"

Maddie had entered her father's house through the patio doors. Voices from the study drew her to the open doorway, where Morgan's voice washed over her like a lover's caress. It took a moment for their words to register in her exhausted brain. *Babies!* They were talking about babies! Four of them to be precise, two girls and two boys! Her babies. Her and Morgan's babies. Precious babies that weren't going to be.

She stepped into her father's study and stared at the two men she loved most in life. After her mother had died, she hadn't known how to protect her heart and stop loving her father. Morgan was a different story. Morgan had snuck up on her when she had been least expecting it. With his profound dark eyes and rough voice he had wormed his way through a crack in the protective wall surrounding her heart.

She watched as both men congratulated each other on the fairy-tale ending that wasn't going to happen. "Father, there aren't going to be any grandchildren." She addressed her father because it was too difficult to face Morgan. She had told him once she wouldn't marry him. She didn't know if she possessed the strength to do it again.

Glen and Morgan jerked around and faced her. "Maddie!" Glen said. "We didn't hear you come in."

"Obviously." She bit her lower lip and kept her gaze on her father. He had been so happy lately. She didn't want to be the one to dull that happiness.

Glen appeared slightly embarrassed at being caught discussing his pending grandchildren. "Can I ask why there won't be any grandchildren?"

"Morgan once told me I have an old-fashioned heart. He was right. I don't sit in judgment of other people, but I believe every child should have both a mother and a father. Since I'm not getting married, that makes babies a null and void issue."

"Why won't you marry Morgan?" Glen glanced at Morgan and then back to her. "The man obviously loves you and he tells me that you love him."

She fought a losing battle with her tears as she glanced at Morgan. He looked about as awful as she felt. What was she doing to him, herself, and even her father? Morgan was gazing at her and waiting for her to answer her father's question. He had asked that same question and she had thrown out a couple of excuses that had nothing to do with the truth. It was time for the truth.

She stared down at the hole worn into the toe of her sneaker. "It's not a perfect world."

"No, it's not," Glen said.

The silence in the room felt oppressive. Morgan seemed to be holding his breath, and her father appeared totally baffled by her statement. To a twelve-year-old girl it was even more baffling and frightening. "In a perfect world people wouldn't die."

"No, they wouldn't. It might get crowded, but they wouldn't die." Glen frowned. "Are you referring to anyone in particular, or are you generalizing?"

"A little of both." She swiped the sleeve of her sweatshirt across her eyes. "When Mom died, I was left alone to figure out what it all meant."

"I was there, Maddie," Glen said. "I know how hard it was on all of us."

The tears came harder, but she could see that Morgan had stood and taken a step toward her. "Forgive me, Dad, but you weren't here. You were lost in a whiskey bottle and I couldn't reach you." The faster she swiped at the tears, the faster they came. She had to get it all out. For once in her life she had to tell her father. "I wanted to join Mom, but I didn't know how. You didn't own a gun and the thought of slicing my wrists made me dizzy." She took a deep breath and told her biggest secret. "I decided on pills."

Here's Lookin' at You

"My God!" Glen exclaimed as he buried his face in his hands.

"One night while you were passed out downstairs, I gathered up all that was left of Mom's pills. You kept her room as a shrine, so they were easy to find. There were eighty-seven pills in a rainbow of colors and all different sizes. Three nights in a row I lined them up and counted each and every one of them."

Morgan moved next to her. "Why didn't you take them, Maddie?" He looked pale and upset, but she could tell he knew. He knew she hadn't taken any of them.

"I had a dream." She stood next to her father and placed a trembling hand upon his shoulder. "Mom was in the dream and she told me to flush all the pills down the toilet." She used her other sleeve to wipe her tears. Her father's head was bent against her hand and she could feel his tears. "Mom told me that you had to work through your grief, Dad. She told me to give you time and that you loved me very much."

"God, I'm sorry, lass," Glen whispered.

"It's okay, Dad. I asked Mom how to grieve. You had your whiskey and work. I had to go to school and face sympathetic looks from teachers and awkward silences from kids who had no concept of what it was like to lose a mother. Mom told me that everyone grieved for a loved one in their own way. That's when I told her I was never going to love anyone ever again."

Morgan reached out and caught one of her tears on the tip of his finger. "What did your mother say to that?"

"She told me I didn't have to love anyone if I didn't want to as long as I flushed the pills and promised not to try anything like that again."

"You flushed the pills, didn't you?" Morgan asked. A light of understanding had entered his eyes.

She nodded. "I flushed the pills."

Two days later Maddie bustled around the cottage as if she were Martha Stewart and the *Today* show was about to make an appearance. In reality, it was Morgan who was about to come for dinner. At least she hoped so. She had called his office during a break in rehearsal and left a message with his secretary that dinner would be ready by six. It would have been, too, if rehearsal hadn't run over. The director had decided that since the rehearsal had gone so well, they might as well stay at it for another hour.

She barely had time for a quick shower and to pick up three days' worth of newspapers messing up the living room. Bird seed was still scattered beneath the parrots' cages and the bathroom should have been condemned. Dinner was downgraded from lasagna to spaghetti, salad, and the loaf of Italian bread she had just yanked from the freezer. The bottle of red cabernet she had picked up on her mad dash home was sitting on the counter.

The minute hand of the clock on the kitchen wall ticked its way to the twelve. Six o'clock. Morgan wasn't coming. She lowered herself onto one of the chairs and stared at the big-faced clock. He had given up on her, washed his hands of everything. Her revelation in her father's study had been too much for him. Morgan now knew her deepest secret, and he couldn't accept the fact that twenty years ago she had been eighty-seven pills away from taking her life.

After she had admitted to Morgan and her father that she had flushed the pills, Morgan had left. He had pulled her into his arms, kissed her on the forehead, told her he now understood and that she should talk to her father. She had thought Morgan was the most considerate man she had ever met, and loved him more for it.

She and her father had talked way into the night. They had touched on every subject, from her mother to the new woman in his life. Every time they had discussed the pills and how close she had come to taking them, her father broke down and cried. Over and over again he told her how sorry he was for not being there when she'd needed him the most. It took a while, but her father slowly started to believe her when she kept telling him she didn't blame him. That night she stayed at her father's house and slept in her old bedroom.

With the dawning of a new day, Glen had taken a couple of hours away from the office and they visited her mother's grave. They had sat together on a white concrete bench watching the fall leaves tumble to the ground. The healing had begun.

Her father had driven her to a little family restaurant on the outskirts of Blue Ball for breakfast. There he brought up Morgan's name. He told her life was nothing but chances and risks. If she stuck with her decision not to get married and forced Morgan from her life, then she and Morgan both lost. But, if she took a chance on their love, they both might win. Over oatmeal, toast, orange juice, and decaf coffee she asked her father only one question. If he'd had a choice and known the outcome, would he have loved her mother all over again. Her father never hesitated. He smiled and said he wouldn't have missed it for the world.

She had gone to rehearsal that day thinking about his words, then spent the entire evening posing inane questions to her parrots. Would she, knowing she would lose Carolyn when she was twelve, have wanted a different mother, one who might have lived longer and still be around today? The answer came as quickly as her father's had, and was the same. She wouldn't have missed being Carolyn's daughter for anything in the world. By one in the morning she had to agree with José and Manuel, she was indeed a hamster brain.

Maddie shook her head to clear it and glanced

again at the clock. Fifteen after six. Morgan was never late for anything in his life. He wasn't coming. Her tear-filled gaze landed on the bottle of wine that wouldn't be opened in celebration. What did she expect? The man had asked her to become his wife, and she'd turned him down.

He had sent her enough flowers to fill a greenhouse and an iron replica of the Maltese Falcon, and she had never even thanked him. Morgan had even gone through the trouble of locating three of Bogey's movies and sending them to her. She knew he had to have watched *To Have and Have Not* because of his note. She'd cried when she read it and ended up with such a bad case of the hiccups, she couldn't have whistled if her life depended upon it.

None of that mattered now. What mattered was that she loved Morgan and was willing to take a risk on that love. She wanted a future as Mrs. Morgan De Witt and she wanted to fill their home with the laughter of children.

She angrily dabbed at her tears with a tissue. She'd be damned before she allowed Morgan just to slip out of her life. If he wouldn't come to her, then she would go to him.

She hurried to the bedroom to check her appearance one last time. The flowing skirt and blouse had seemed like a good choice half an hour ago, but now she wasn't sure. Maybe she should change into something a little sexier. Morgan seemed to have liked the green silk dress she had worn to her father's engagement party. In fact, he'd liked it so well he couldn't wait to get her out of it. The dress had spent the night lying on a kitchen chair if her memory served her right.

She gave the closet door a good yank and pushed hangers aside, looking for the green silk. A frown pulled at her mouth as she surveyed the wrinkled dress. It looked like it had spent the night jammed under the refrigerator, not tossed over a chair. She replaced the hanger and glared at the remaining clothes. Morgan had once told her that Yewanna Synne could seduce him anytime. She was tempted to try, but she didn't have anything that even remotely resembled an Elizabethan vixen's outfit. She missed working at the Pennsylvania Renaissance Faire, but they had closed for the season. Mark, the staff director, had promised her a job next summer when it started back up again. Until then there were plenty of other places for her to work.

She closed the closet door and stared at her reflection in the mirror. What she was wearing would have to do. She started for the living room just as someone knocked on her front door. Morgan! She ran to the door and her hand trembled as she yanked it open.

Morgan stood on her doorstep. A Morgan she had never seen before. His hands were filthy and two of his knuckles appeared to be bleeding. He didn't have on his suit jacket or even a tie, and his white silk shirt was smeared with dirt and grease, as was one side of his face. Even the knees of his pants were dirty and she could no longer see her reflection in his shoes. "What happened to you?" She grabbed his arm and pulled him into the house.

"Flat tire." He raised his hand to brush back a lock of hair and glared at the dirt covering it. "Can I use the bathroom to clean up?"

"Of course." She lifted his hand and frowned at the bleeding knuckles. They didn't appear too bad, just scraped up. "What did you do, punch the flat tire off?"

"Just about." Morgan studied her face. "You're not mad that I ruined dinner?"

She smiled. "I didn't even start it yet. I was late getting home, rehearsal ran over." He had looked so worried about being late. "You go take a shower, and I'll start dinner."

"Let me get the change of clothes that I carry in the trunk of my car."

He looked so serious, she just had to tease him. "Hoping to get lucky?"

"No. I carry them in case I'm away from the office and I'm needed on a job site. It's only jeans and a flannel shirt, but they're better than what I have on." He glanced down at his ruined shirt and pants. "I can't even sit on your couch with these on." He opened the door and headed for his car.

Maddie stood in the kitchen and listened as Morgan reentered the house and headed for the bathroom. A minute later the shower started. She picked up the box of noodles and weighed her options. She could cook a mediocre meal and bore Morgan with her domestic abilities. Or she could go join him in the shower and offer to scrub his back. The box of noodles landed on the counter with a satisfying thud.

Morgan felt the draft as the shower curtain was pushed aside and Maddie stepped into the tub. A deliciously naked Maddie. "What do you think you're doing?" He was on the verge of pinning her to the green tiled wall and taking her right there. Didn't she realize how much control it had cost him not to haul her into his arms the second she opened her door? He had spent an hour that afternoon sitting at his desk staring at the pink phone message and grinning. *While you were out: Maddie called. Dinner at six.* There was only one reason Maddie would have left that message: She was ready to step into the future, their future.

She reached for his hand and examined the scraped knuckles once again. "I'm playing doctor." Her fingers trailed up his forearm. "Are you hurt anywhere else?"

He shuddered as heat slammed into his body. His desire for Maddie pooled in one very obvious place. "Oh, I'm hurting all right, but it's not something a doctor can fix."

Here's Lookin' at You

Her fingers stroked his chest and headed downward. "Let me be the judge of that one."

He captured her hand before it completed its journey. If she touched him, it would be all over. He'd have her pressed against the tile so fast, the fish on the shower curtain would fry from the friction. "Come on, Maddie, I'm trying to be a gentleman here."

"If I had wanted a gentleman, I would have gone to the country club." She pressed her mouth against his chest. "You're the one who told me anytime I wanted something, all I had to do was whistle." She glanced up as her mouth slid lower. "I know how to whistle, Morgan." Her eyes sparkled with pure mischief as she went lower still. "All I have to do is put my lips together and blow."

He couldn't prevent the laugh that ripped through his throat as he hauled her up straight and captured her seductive mouth. He could feel the cool tile against the palms of his hands as he backed her against the tub wall. Warm water pelted them both as he entered her with one powerful thrust. He wasn't positive, but he could have sworn he smelled frying fish.

An hour later they sat cuddled on the couch drinking wine and eating Italian bread smeared with peanut butter. Maddie licked her finger and grinned. "Really, Morgan, I wouldn't have minded cooking dinner."

He nuzzled her neck. "Forget it, this is much better. I don't want you out of my arms."

She wasn't about to argue with him. Now that she was back in them, she might never leave. "What's your opinion about New Year's Day?"

He took a sip of wine and shrugged. "Quiet day, nothing much happening. Everyone recovering from the night before."

"I think it's perfect."

"Okay, it's perfect." His lips skimmed her ear as his free hand ventured inside the lapel of her robe. His fingers cupped her breast. "Perfect for what?"

She pressed against his warm bare chest. After they'd finally made it out of the bathroom in barely one piece, she had tugged on her robe—her hideous robe—and Morgan had stepped into his jeans. "Perfect for our wedding day."

Morgan's hand stilled. "Really, Maddie? Are you sure?" He released her breast and cupped her chin as he studied her face. "I won't rush you, Slim. I love you so much, but I want you to be absolutely sure."

She stroked his cheek. "I'm absolutely, positively sure, Morgan. I love you, and I want to be your wife and the mother of your children."

His mouth lowered and his kiss was as sweet and loving as summer rain.

Here's Lookin' at You
209

"Friends, Romans, countrymen, lend me your ears," screamed José.

"Lovers to bed; 'tis almost fairy time," answered Manuel.

She felt Morgan stiffen and then chuckle. "Don't laugh," she said. "It only encourages them."

"Off with her head! Grawwwwk, off with her head!"

"A horse! A horse! My kingdom for a horse!"

"Long live the queen!"

"This blessed plot, this earth, this realm, this England!" shouted José.

"Long live the queen! Off with her head! Long live the queen," cried Manuel.

Morgan roared with laughter. "My God, he's schizophrenic."

She playfully punched him on the arm. "He is not. They don't understand the words, only how to say them." She stood up and headed for the cages. "It's their bedtime."

"I never did hear what you taught José to sing."

She grinned as she approached José's cage. "Pretty boy, José. Sing for Maddie. Sing pretty."

José cocked his head, ruffled up his feathers, and for once listened to her. In his screechy voice, he sang the first verse of "As Time Goes By."

Morgan rose from the couch and wrapped his arms around her, swaying with her as José belted out the last line. Maddie could feel her eyes get all misty.

Morgan brushed a kiss on top of her head and smiled at the parrot. "Play it again, Sam."

José made a rude sound back at him. "José, José, José!" He gave a little shake of his head and muttered, "Hamster brain."

EPILOGUE

Morgan smiled as he entered the White Lace and Promises Bridal Boutique. Then again, he had been doing nothing but smiling lately. In three very long weeks, he was going to become a married man. A very happy married man. His smile grew as the sound of voices carried to him from the back fitting room. He picked out Maddie's immediately, and his sister's too. One of the voices belonged to Brenda and the rest of the chatter had to be the assorted assistants that buzzed around the boutique like little bees.

He glanced around the shop and frowned at the window display. There wasn't any. A naked mannequin with a crooked red wig stood in the center of the boutique. He was half tempted to throw something on her and give her at least a smidgen of pride.

"Mr. De Witt," exclaimed Cleo, the owner, as

she hurried from the back room. The rose-colored curtain fluttered in her wake. "Mademoiselle Andrews told me you would be stopping by." Cleo clutched her hands to her chest. "She is exquisite. She will be the most beautiful bride."

He grinned. "Of that I have no doubt." He gazed at the curtain separating him from his fiancée. "Is everything going okay? Did Maddie find a dress she liked?" He didn't know why he was so worried. Maddie seemed to know exactly what kind of wedding she wanted. As far as he was concerned a quick trip to Vegas or a justice of the peace would serve the purpose. But if Maddie wanted a fancy wedding, by hell she was going to get a fancy wedding.

"Your bride-to-be knew exactly what she wanted before stepping a foot in the door."

Maddie's sweet laughter caught and held his attention. As the sound of it drifted away, he turned back to Cleo. "I want her happy, Cleo. Whatever she wants, give it to her and send me the bill."

"No, Mr. De Witt. Her father has made all the arrangements." Cleo straightened the wig on the naked mannequin and clicked her tongue. "Madeline Andrews is not only happy, she is radiant." Cleo turned to him and smiled. "That, I believe, has more to do with you than my exquisite creation, which she is currently being fit for."

He nodded. What he really felt like doing was pounding on his chest and announcing to the

Here's Lookin' at You

world that he, Morgan De Witt, had made Madeline Andrews radiant. "Did my sister also find something?" He had been pleased that Georgia and Maddie's childhood friendship had resumed after so many years without missing a beat. Maddie had insisted that Georgia act as matron of honor.

"Yes, oh my, yes," Cleo answered. "It's a magnificent gown of midnight blue. A little gather here and a little gather there, and it will fit perfectly."

Morgan chuckled, knowing exactly where the gathers were going to be. Georgia and Levi had announced their news at Glen and Brenda's wedding reception. He couldn't have been happier to learn he was going to become an uncle.

"Mr. De Witt, may I ask you a question?"

"Go ahead."

"Are there any more De Witts at home? My business has sure picked up since meeting you."

Morgan threw back his head and roared with laughter.

THE EDITORS' CORNER

It's hard to believe that autumn is here! Soon Old Man Winter will be making his way down our paths, and we'll all be complaining about the cold weather instead of the oppressive heat. One thing you won't be complaining about is the Loveswept November lineup. And trust us, Old Man Winter doesn't stand a chance with these sexy men on the prowl!

Timing is everything, so they say, and Suzanne Brockmann proves the old adage true with her next LOVESWEPT, #858, **TIME ENOUGH FOR LOVE**. Chuck Della Croce has a problem. His time machine is responsible for a tragedy that has resulted in the deaths of hundreds. Thinking he can go back in time to literally save the world, Chuck ends up on Maggie Winthrop's doorstep. Maggie can't help but notice the stranger who's obnoxiously banging on her door, especially since he's naked as a jaybird! When he tells her he's from the future, she's ready to call the men in white coats, but something about him gives her pause. As Chuck explains his mission to prevent a disaster and save her life, Maggie must learn to accept that anything is possible. Suzanne Brockmann guides us in a timeless journey and persuades us to believe in the powers of destiny and second chances.

Eyes meeting across a crowded room, sexual tension building to a crescendo . . . *bam!*, you've got yourself a Loveswept! That certainly is the recipe conjured up in LOVESWEPT #859, **RELATIVE STRANGERS**, by Kathy Lynn Emerson. A ghost is lurking in the halls of Sinclair House, one who is anxious to reunite with her own true love. But first she must bring together the hearts of Lucas Sinclair and Corrie Ballantyne. Unfortunately, the two won't cooperate. Strange occurrences involving Corrie keep happening at Lucas's historic hotel, and he needs to get to the bottom of things before the place goes under. After seeing the ghosts of Lucas's ancestors, Corrie must decide if it's her own desire that draws her to him, or if it's the will of another. Can Corrie make peace with the past by unearthing hidden truths and soothing the unspoken sorrows of the man she will love forever? Kathy Lynn Emerson's exquisitely romantic ghost story is downright irresistible in both its sensuality and its mystery.

Trapped on an island with a hurricane on the loose, Trevor Fox and Jana Jenkins seek **SHELTER FROM THE STORM**, LOVESWEPT #860 by Maris Soule. Cursing a storm that had grounded all his charters, Trevor was only too glad to agree to lend a hand to the alluring seductress with the pouty lips.

Little did he know that his day would go from bad to worse, and from there to . . . well, whatever comes after that. Held at gunpoint, he is forced to fly to the Bahamas, and into the path of a hurricane. Jana Jenkins just wants to live a quiet, uneventful life, but when her stepbrother is kidnapped, Jana does what's necessary to save him—even if that includes dragging this brash pirate with a tarnished reputation along for the ride. Loveswept veteran Maris Soule knows there's nothing like a little danger to spice up the lives of a woman on the run and a man who enjoys the chase!

Dr. Kayla Davies learns just what will be her **ULTIMATE SURRENDER**, LOVESWEPT #861 by Jill Shalvis, an author who is penning her way into our hearts. When Kayla and her ex–brother-in-law, Ryan Scott, are summoned to the home of a beloved aunt, the two must make peace with their past and with each other. There's no love lost between the ruthless police detective and Kayla, but Ryan can't understand the fear he sees lurking in the depths of her blue eyes. As Kayla grows to know Ryan, she finds herself in the strange position of being both attracted and repelled by the man she once believed evil. Trapped in a web of old deceits, Ryan and Kayla struggle together to silence the ghosts of their past. But if Kayla dares to confess her dark secret, can Ryan find the strength to forgive? Writing with touching emotion and tender sensuality, Jill Shalvis once again proves that love can be a sweet victory over heartbreak.

Happy reading!

With warmest regards,

Susann Brailey
Senior Editor

Joy Abella
Administrative Editor